*The Fog Comes on Little Pig Feet*

# The Fog Comes on Little Pig Feet

## Rosemary Wells

*Illustrations by the author*

*The Dial Press*  *New York*

Library of Congress Cataloging in Publication Data

Wells, Rosemary.
  The fog comes on little pig feet.

  Summary: Hating the boarding school where she is sent against
her wishes, a thirteen-year-old finds her rebellion getting her
in increasingly deeper trouble.
  [1.  School stories]  I.  Title.
PZ7.W46843Fo  [Fic]  71-37622

*For Hrair B.*

*The Fog Comes on Little Pig Feet*

## Sunday, September 30

*FOUR THOUSAND DOLLARS!* Now that I've written it down, it seems a little less frightening. Saying it aloud makes me feel all weak in the stomach. I finally got Mother and Dad to tell me how much school is going to cost. There was an awful silence in the room when Mother said the words. She just stared down at the slipcover and folded it in and out of her fingers. Daddy cleared his throat, as if he were about to comment, but I had already left the room. I know it bothers them dreadfully when I leave in the middle of a conversation or simply refuse to reply, but sometimes I can't help it. It feels just as if an invisible hand comes out of the blue and sweeps me away before I have a chance to say anything.

Swamp followed me down to the beach. He's a very sensible dog and listens solemnly when I have no one else to talk to.

"Where did they get four thousand dollars, Swamp?" I asked him. Swamp said nothing but looked morose. "They must have borrowed it from a bank. Banks are big on education and stuff like that. That means they're in debt on my account." No answer.

The beach in back of our apartment building is a lovely place to be alone. I can sing down there and work out music that I've written. No one can hear. I haven't told anyone I've begun to compose yet. And I'd just die if anyone caught me conducting. I love to pretend the New York Philharmonic is sitting before me, playing my favorite parts from symphonies. Once every so often, when I really get going conducting and singing, Swamp can be induced to howl. That is quite sensational.

But tonight I wished I'd had more than just Swamp to talk to, and I wished I hadn't left the house so abruptly. Mother and Dad do try. They ask me "Rachel, what's on your mind?" or "I hope if anything's bothering you, you'll come to us." Sometimes, when Mother is dusting or looking in the other direction, she'll tell me that if I ever get into trouble to remember that they'll be there and never to go to strangers, but I always clam up when they say those things.

I can't even talk to Linda McCarthy about boarding school. (Not that we have any secrets between us, just things we can't discuss. For instance, the fact that she is a Catholic and I am nothing.) Linda definitely senses how Mother feels about public school and, for that matter, how she feels about people in general. Public school in Brooklyn isn't good enough for me, Mother is always saying, so I have to go away to private school "in a country environment." Apparently I will meet people there who will matter to me all my life, "nice girls from nice families," whatever that means. I wouldn't mind so much if they sent me to a music school, but Mother says she doesn't want me associating with "arty types" exclusively, and Dad says I will have a marvelous education in the next four years and get into the college of my choice. Linda has never actually heard them say these things, because they are careful around her, but she knows all the same. She has been going to high school two weeks now and loves it. I can't get it out of my head that Linda is gone for good, and that somehow I deserve this. I called the Pope a troublemaker in front of her two years ago. Linda told me I'd go to hell for that remark, so I said she was just an old bead rattler. Later she forgave me, but I've never forgiven myself. Why do I have to remember things like that right now?

Swamp kept running off after his own particular phantoms tonight and was not much company. I didn't want to call him back too often or too loud. Hearing your own voice hang in the air is frightening when it catches. . . . But as a treat, for its being my last night home, Saint Elmo's lights came along the shore. Tiny phosphorus creatures floating gently in the wavelets, getting all over my foot and ankle. Had I dunked my whole self in the ocean, I do believe I would have looked like one of those drawings of a constellation, but with millions of stars instead of seven or eight. I read once, in *Moby Dick*, that sailors consider Saint Elmo's lights a terrible omen. There's a part where the *Pequod* is caught in a typhoon. One night Saint Elmo's appear all over the rigging and harpoons, scaring all hell out of the crew.

At any rate, the blue lights put me in mind of a time when I was very little. Mother and Dad and I had gone down to the beach in New Jersey for a picnic on a late summer evening like this. The lights came on in the ocean, and Mother let me take off my bathing suit and romp in the waves. Every new wave brought another shower of silver over me, and soon I was covered from head to foot. After a bit, Mother took off her suit too, smiling at Daddy, and then he took off all his clothes and dived into the sea, whooping and shouting like a kid. They splashed each other with sprays of the lights and splashed me and held me up for the other to see. Then Daddy said he had to catch the last of the bass, since they were running that night like he'd never seen them run before. He put on his pants and gathered up his fishing equipment. Every once in a while Mother called down to the end of the jetty, "Bill, are you all right?" and he'd whistle back very low, so as not to disturb the fish.

Mother and I stayed on the beach, watching the last of the fire burn down to brilliant orange ashes. We stared at the shapes the crumbling logs made as they fell down on one another. There were houses and people and strange characters out of German operas. I remember distinctly a dwarf beating a drum in a doorway. "Mother, do you see him!" I whispered. "Yes," she said, "and he has a hat with three bells on top." It's quite something when you can see the same things in ashes as somebody else.

"Swamp came back," Dad announced stiffly and interrupted my dreaming. We walked back to the house together. Dad tried to put his arm around my shoulders, but I skipped to the side, feeling terrible as I did, but I hate embarrassing scenes.

"You mustn't take it too hard, Rache. We all have to leave home sometime," he said.

I fumbled for something to say. He sounded so dreadfully final. I half expected one of his Walt Disney nature-film lectures about salmon swimming upstream or the redwing blackbirds migrating to Tanganyika for the berry season. He always brings up nature when he's explaining a point to me. Apparently we are all "part of a grand design." But he said nothing this time.

"There's a difference between leaving and being sent," I muttered at last.

"Now you're acting like a child. You have to be a little more grown-up about these things."

"Grown-ups aren't sent places unless they go to jail. If a grown-up leaves, it's because he's made up his own mind."

"That's not altogether true, honey. Life isn't a bowl of cherries for anyone." Dad was verging on a reference to the old country. Whenever he wants me to do something, he mentions his boyhood in Armenia. Whether it's the oatmeal I have to eat in the morning that he would have given his eyeteeth for as a boy, or the education I'm about to get at North Place, it's all the same. At least Mother's on my side in this. She's gotten him to stop saying "I got my education in the school of hard knocks." She also tries to stop him from calling Europe "across the pond" and from washing the car with his old underwear. She is unsuccessful in the last two.

"Just give it a chance, honey," he pleaded. "You'll

be glad someday that you didn't stay in Brooklyn."

"I could have gone to Music and Art in Manhattan," I argued. "Miss Tully says I could get in easily."

"Rache," he began, and we both knew he'd said it all before, "this is going to be a broadening experience. Believe me, I know what I'm talking about. Playing the piano is a wonderful thing to do, and if someday you can play well enough to make some money, that's fine. But you can't depend on that. Miss Tully is a fine woman, but you don't want to end up just teaching piano to kids. Think of the world of opportunity open to you with a good education in English and science and a college degree, too."

"But I'm not *interested* in English and science."

"Honey, you're too young now. You don't know yet. Maybe you'll marry a rich guy someday and never have to worry, but at least we can be sure you'll have a chance at a career you'll be proud of."

"I'd be proud of being a musician!"

"Sure. Charley Finley is a fine musician. He even plays in groups, but you notice he makes good money in his job too. He has both."

I wanted to say "Charley Finley—yecch!" but I'd have hurt Dad terribly, because Charley is Dad's best friend. We had reached the door by this time anyway, and Dad was looking sheepish. I think he knew he'd hit the sore point again. I'm not sure I have the ability to be a professional pianist either, but I'd like to try.

"Tight sleep, Piglet," he said as I dashed upstairs.

"Yeah," I shouted back. He hadn't called me Piglet in four years. I undressed immediately. They don't come in anymore if I'm naked, particularly Daddy. So if I want to be unbothered I simply take my clothes off.

I caught myself looking in the mirror. I *hate* mirrors. They make me look so gawky. Dear God, please make this a stage I'm going through. Thirteen years old, thirty-seven pubic hairs. Linda has over seventy and has stopped counting, but that's because she's Irish and they develop faster. I closed my eyes to the mirror, but it was too late. Whenever I badger myself about being flat-chested, skinny, pigeon-toed, and wearing glasses, my Choice Genie swoops down and · says, "Would you rather have over a hundred pubic hairs and a 36C bra, or be able to play the piano and get a fine education?"

Naturally I opt for the piano and the education. If I don't, I know I'll be ignorant for the rest of my life and go to high school in Brighton Beach and, as Mother says, "marry some soldier."

Superstitions, like flying needles, keep at me tonight. I wonder if Saint Elmo's lights really are a bad omen. How about book burning? Today I bought a copy of *The Count of Monte Cristo*, in French, tore out the pages carefully, and threw them in an incinerator. Then I glued the pages of this diary into the empty cover.

No one will be likely to pick up a book with *Le Comte de Monte Cristo* on the spine. Someday I intend to read the real *Count of Monte Cristo*—part of the bargain for keeping a diary secret! I do hope I don't make myself read it in French.

## Monday, October 1

I am sitting in one of the lavatories in the dorm, which, I hope, is kept lit all night long. The outside door is marked GIRLS, as if there might be a boy lurking about! I'm positive no male has ever set foot in these halls, save a cheery father or two bringing suitcases up to the rooms, and everyone knows cheery fathers never go to the bathroom. The tubs, where I am writing, and most of the johns are closed in with wooden partitions. Some of the johns are not, however. I wonder who uses them?

Some reassurance does come from these funny old-fashioned partitions, behind which, as last resort, everyone can just be herself. The schedule we are asked to live by here affords so little free time, and when free time is allowed, it's almost always arranged to be spent in the presence of others, so I've decided that sitting in this cubicle is the only way to be alone.

This diary is bothering me slightly. Daddy has a John Wayneish way of saying "You're a loner, Rachel," which is all very fine for cowboys, but probably not so fine for teen-age girls. People who talk to themselves are supposed to be crazy. Having a diary is "normal," but in a way it is talking to myself. I am afraid, at times, that I shall be the first in my family to go mad. For instance, things bother me from years past. Mostly embarrassing or stupid things. They pass through my head like unseen spaceships showing up as *blips* on a radar screen, until I work myself through them again, feel the heebie-jeebies or the humiliation one more time, and then they go away. One is passing over right now. Last semester I was sitting in English class, killing time with Sue Fazio, whose brother happens to be the most popular and sensational-looking guy in the whole eighth grade (probably in the whole high school by now). She told me that instead of getting skin trouble at puberty, Lenny's teeth had all fallen out. That was interesting. I hadn't even known he'd reached puberty. Anyway, I just happened to meet him in the hall after class, and I, who had never dared even to speak to him since sixth grade, said "Hi, Lenny. How are your teeth?"

He turned bright red and walked away. Why did I say that? Why why why why why??????????

I'll begin again with today. A total loss. Mother and Dad had what I call "the fun conversation" in the front seat of the car. That's the one where they talk about all the fun I'm going to have at North Place. I am to make many friends. Some of them will have houses in the country as well as in the city. Some even will have houses in foreign countries. (I can't imagine somebody having more than one house. They'd have to cart all their favorite things all over the lot. "George, where's that copy of *Crime and Punishment*?" "I'm sorry, dear, it's in the Newport house. You'll have to read *War and Peace* instead.")

Mother also said that I'll probably be spending a great many vacations with these people. I will learn to ski, play tennis, ride, and do all sorts of things I wouldn't have the opportunity to do in New York City. I said that they had riding and skiing at Van Cortlandt Park in the Bronx.

"Van Cortlandt Park!" Mother trumpeted. "Van Cortlandt *Park*!"

"There's nothing wrong with Van Cortlandt Park," Daddy broke in. "You're going to make a snob out of her, Jessica."

"I meant that I really want to come home for vacations," I said meekly, trying to make peace.

Mother changed the subject. "Rachel, what's in that brown paper bag?"

"My penguin."

"Your penguin! It isn't even clean!"

"Let her have it if she wants it," Daddy said.

"Everybody wants something from home with them when they go to a strange place."

That's quite true, of course, although I didn't admit it to them. All my clothes except my sneakers are brand-new. Even my toothbrush and hairbrush and that stupid plastic soap dish are new, and they feel as if they belong to somebody else. I hadn't looked at my penguin in at least five years till this morning when I suddenly fished him out of the back of the closet. He isn't too clean, as a matter of fact, and he has a Merthiolate stain on his chest and is missing one glass eye, but I don't care. If anyone asks me who he is, I'll say my boyfriend Pete won him for me in an amusement park this summer. (I do know two Petes.)

Little things were terribly different today. It made me remember the first day I wore glasses, when everything looked just slightly wonky and I kept noticing queer details. I counted the mileage signs on the Connecticut Turnpike. I wanted them to be posted at least two miles apart to lengthen the trip. We passed a billboard with two giant cow heads sticking out of it, advertising a dairy company. I've never seen a three-dimensional billboard before, and I know it would have delighted me on any other day. But this morning it seemed ominous, a landmark from here on in of halfway from home. I do believe that three-dimensional billboards will jolt me from this day forth.

MATTAPEQUOT 1 MILE, BOSTON 10 MILES said a sign,

and we were almost there. By this time I'd gone into a complete fog. My parents were still chattering, but there might as well have been a pane of glass between the front seat and the back. I imagined for a moment I was riding in an old limousine with a chauffeur's partition and was half tempted to reach out and rap it with my knuckles but stopped myself in time.

I squeezed my eyes shut and just wished North Place off the face of the earth. That is not quite as silly as it sounds. Somewhere in Europe there is a woman who bleeds from her feet, hands, and side every Thursday at one o'clock. People come from all over to see her and pray, and all because she once spotted the Virgin Mary next to a stream. Miracles do happen.

Daddy got lost, as usual, and wouldn't ask his way. He always does this, preferring to circle like a buzzard looking for a mouse. This time, however, Mother would not let up on him and made him ask directions at a gas station. The attendant gave our car a second look before he answered. Later I noticed we had the only ten-year-old Ford in the school parking lot. Mercedes Benzes, Cadillacs, unidentifiables, but no Fords.

A "tea thing," as Mother had predicted, was going on in the lobby of the main building. Parents, girls, and brothers were all madly carrying suitcases and boxes upstairs to the dormitory. They all had to go through a checkpoint first, where they were greeted by Miss Pick, the headmistress, and her sidekick, a very fat lady with a purple birthmark running down the side of her neck and into her cleavage.

The lobby is cavernous, with at least ten groupings of straight-backed chairs and spindly tables against the walls. On each table rests a silver bowl filled with straw flowers of the school colors, green and gold, and above every table is an oil painting of an old person. I doubt if the chairs are ever used. I'd be afraid of turning into a piece of furniture myself if I ever sat down in one.

We shook hands and said "How do you do" to Miss Pick. Daddy forgot her name, but she didn't appear to notice. She continued whatever she had been saying and indicated, with an upturned hand like a mannequin, the fat birthmark lady on her right, who was working a samovar. "And this is Miss Abloi," said Miss Pick.

"So glad to meet you, Rachel," Miss Abloi chirped. "Mr. and Mrs. Sa . . . Saseekian's."

"And what have you in your bag, Rachel?" asked Miss Pick, twinkling a little at me.

"A penguin, ma'am," I said, looking down at my feet. I said nothing about boys or amusement parks.

"Wonderful!" grinned Miss Pick. "Just so long as it isn't a flashlight."

"A flashlight?" Mother asked.

"Some of our girls take to reading after lights-out," explained Miss Pick with another grin, and she started greeting the next family.

The school building is very much like an old hotel,

the kind where you find gas lamps turned electric and sinks in the bedrooms. All the dormitory corridors look exactly alike, and we marched up and down for twenty minutes trying to find Room 40, Daddy, carrying the suitcases, swearing softly under his breath. I had to touch the wallpaper. It had fuzzy patches of gold flowers all over it, like a greeting card, but Mother told me to keep my hands off or the acid from my fingers would ruin it.

Once again I made a wish. This time that there would simply be no Room 40, and I would have to go home for at least one more night. The Choice Genie flickered briefly into my wish. "Do you want to run away and be a coward for the rest of your days, or would you rather be brave and possibly get invited to a Princeton weekend someday?" he asked. I tried to block him by picturing Dorothy being swept out of Kansas into Emerald City, but the Choice Genie is persistent. He always makes me do what I most loathe, face things I wouldn't ordinarily face. "*The Wizard of Oz* is a children's book," he warned. "You have to be grown-up now." At that moment Room 40 appeared. On the door was a metal bracket with two names stamped in plastic, mine and E. Faber's; the first thing that did not remind me of an old hotel.

I was furious when I saw my name on the door. I ripped out the plastic panel and threw it on the floor. Mother replaced it wordlessly, only giving me a dark look. I do feel that you ought to be able to control what happens to your name.

E. Faber had arrived but was not in sight. She'd already claimed the best bed and bureau and had put her stuff all around the room. I put my penguin and my piano scores on the bed. Mother was already unpacking and hanging things in the closet. I just sat. Daddy said he'd be "better off downstairs." I looked at him quickly and said, "Don't leave, promise!"

"Of course not," he said. "I'll just be down there among all the old biddies."

I knew, of course, that he couldn't leave just like that. I don't know why I said it, except that my heart felt like an oyster inside me.

There was a cardinal bouncing around on a pine tree outside the window. He looked so free as he darted from branch to branch, and he could go home anytime he wished. I began to picture myself one-inch tall, riding on his back between his wings. A small boy, Little Diamond was his name, I believe, once took off on the back of the North Wind. I have a picture of him on a book cover at home, holding tight to the enormous black tresses of the North Wind, flying over a night countryside dotted with faraway lights.

"Rachel, will you please try and look a little more cheerful," said Mother, pushing the hair off her forehead. "Here I've done all the unpacking, and you're just sitting on the bed mooning."

"I'm sorry," I said.

"Really, honey, I don't mind so much, and I know how you feel, but you're making Daddy and I feel dreadful by being so sad. We don't want you to be away from home any more than you do."

"Then why do I have to be?"

"Rachel," she said, half exasperated, half warning.

"I'm sorry."

"Honey, we've saved and saved for this. You *know* that. We want you to have better than us. We've forgone a new car and a lot of other things. I don't expect you to understand this fully, but please stop making us feel we've done wrong."

"I'm sorry."

"Well then," she began, in a "that's settled" voice, "I brought you these, just in case."

"*Mother!*" I felt myself turning scarlet. Mother waved a box of Kotex around in the air. Although I'm just thirteen, one of my secret shames is that I have not yet "reached puberty," as they say. I certainly don't want anybody to know. If my roommate sees an unopened box of Kotex in my closet for three or four months, she'll get suspicious. I can't get rid of them slowly for fear of trapping myself in a hideous embarrassment. I told Mother I could buy them myself.

"Well it won't hurt to have them," she said, "and if you don't use them, you can give them to your roommate."

"Mother, please!" I groaned. "Why do you always have to say things like that?"

"Like what?" she asked. "I thought you'd be pleased if I treated you like a grown-up young lady."

Luckily Mother did not write my name on the box, like she does on everything else, including my lunch at school. I should be able to get rid of them by leaving the box in the girls' room late some night. For the time being, it won't hurt to keep them in the closet.

We looked at the things E. Faber had placed around the room. There was a huge purple-and-yellow panda on the bed, several college pennants, a sign saying "Chicken Little Was Right," and a photograph of a boy, inscribed, "Love, Jack—see the back." but we couldn't see the back because it was in a silver frame.

"Her boyfriend," I announced.

"Sterling silver," said Mother, simultaneously, then she added, "Nonsense, children your age don't have boyfriends." We had no more time for argument, for E. Faber suddenly bounced into the room. She had long dirty-blond hair, a fabulous suntan, and at least a 36 C bra. I disliked her immediately.

"Hi, Rachel!" she said, and once again I was stupidly angry for the bandying about of my name.

"Hi," I said cooly, feeling rotten, because I knew she only wanted to be nice.

But she was already noticing Mother, in a breathless sort of way.

"How do you do."

Mother smiled. "I'm so glad Rachel will have a roommate who knows the ropes, so to speak. I'm sure you two will have a wonderful year together."

I was about to ask Mother what she knew about this girl and what this was about knowing the ropes, but the girl turned, still bubbling with energy, and said, "I'm Ebbie Faber, by the way," and to me she said something about the great times she would be able to show me and how glad she was they put her with a new girl, especially one who was talented. "Maybe some of it'll rub off." She laughed, rolling her eyes and grinning broadly. I haven't any idea how she knew about the piano. Sheets of facts must have circulated about me between my parents and the school without my knowing it.

Mother said it was time to go, and Ebbie winked at me as I left the room.

"Well," said Mother as she flounced downstairs ahead of me, "you certainly weren't very nice to Ebbie."

"What do you mean?"

"You know perfectly well what I mean."

"Well, I just don't like her that much."

"Don't like her?" said Mother, stopping and looking straight up at me, with one hand on the wall and one hand on the banister. "How can you say such a thing when you don't even know her?"

I thought of telling Mother about the acid from her fingers on the wallpaper, but perhaps she has no acid. "Can't I not like someone?" I asked.

"Rachel, listen to me. Ebbie Faber is a darling girl and I want you to try and like her."

"For crying out loud, Mother—"

"And don't use vulgar, rude expressions you pick up from your friends in Brooklyn in a place like this. These girls come from nice families, and it will reflect on Daddy and I if you don't speak properly."

I said nothing but rolled my eyes a bit.

"And don't roll your eyes like that!"

"Ebbie Faber rolled *her* eyes!"

"She most certainly did not," said Mother, "and if she did she didn't do it in a rude way like you."

"That's because she's a royal lunchbox, deep down," I muttered.

"APOLOGIZE FOR THAT REMARK!"

"I apologize."

"Honestly," Mother huffed, going downstairs again, "if it isn't one thing, it's another. You're so critical. I don't know where you get it from except those friends of yours. I want you to promise me you'll try and like Ebbie."

"O.K." I said.

We found Daddy in the very back of the lobby reading a month-old edition of the *Christian Science Monitor*. I almost expected him to be holding it upside down, because he was not concentrating at all. He looked most uncomfortable, being the only man in the room. Miss Pick, Miss Abloi, and the brass samovar were gone. In their place were many middle-aged ladies drinking tea and fluttering. I felt myself fall headfirst into his lapel, and suddenly we were out in the parking lot again, saying good-bye.

"Next weekend!" I shouted at the closed windows of the car. I tried to hold it back by grabbing the rear-door handle. "Next weekend, you promised!"

Daddy stopped. Mother unrolled her window and held my hand. "Honey," she said softly, "we've been over this and over this. If you take next weekend home, you won't be allowed to have another until after Thanksgiving. Why don't you at least get yourself settled and then in three weeks or so you can come home."

"Next weekend!" I insisted with my teeth clenched.

Daddy leaned over and suggested, "How about next Sunday? Supposing we come and visit you next Sunday? How would that be?"

"Next weekend I'm coming *home*!"

"Honey—"

"If you don't want to pick me up, I'll take the bus. I have the money, and—"

"They won't let you, Rache, not without our permission."

"Well *give* it then!"

I let go of the handle and turned my back. I guess they left quickly, because when I looked out of the corner of my eye next, the car was gone. If I am going to cry at all, I want to do it by myself, or if it has to be in front of others, at least in some sort of understandable emergency. I have been on the verge of it all day today. I know it is childish and weak, but it overcomes me like a wave from the sea. "Cry!" I told myself, but I couldn't.

The grounds are so neat, the buildings so perfect. I looked at them closely for the first time walking back from the car. Every hall is made of dark-gray stone, stained with black drips in places and covered with vines and vines of brittle red ivy. There are four turrets on each building, one to a corner, and stone animal faces around the eaves of every turret. The windows are mostly pointed and churchlike, except for the new ones in the kitchen. I could count five enormous halls from where I stood in the driveway. Then there was another a good way off, surrounded by water. I had to laugh at myself, expecting to see Rapunzel in a conical hat letting down her hair from one of the windows, but no such creature appeared. North Place really could have been transported exactly as it is from an old English fairy tale. Even the grass is perfect. Golf grass, I call it.

The front hall was empty when I walked back in.

I wondered what happened to all the twittering old ladies who had been there only ten minutes before. They hadn't even left their teacups. A card table had been set up in the middle of the room. It was stacked with papers and behind it was a gloomy-looking girl reading a large book.

"Got your pamphlet yet?" she asked as I went by.

"No," I said and took one off the top of the pile.

"Freshman?" she asked.

"Yes."

"Better get your uniform on then."

"How come you're not wearing one?" I asked her.

"I'm a senior on honors," she said mournfully, taking a bite out of a peach.

"What language is that?" I asked, looking at the undecipherable title on her book.

"Greek."

"Greek!"

"Homer," she said.

Some of the peach juice dribbled down her chin onto the page, but she didn't bother to sweep it off.

"You mean you're just sitting there reading Homer in Greek!"

"I'm a senior on honors," she said again.

I'm going to slip the first page of the pamphlet into my diary at this point.

## WELCOME TO NORTH PLACE!

If you're an old girl, you'll know your schedule and be familiar with the rules, but do read them anyway. (It's been a long long summer!) If you're new (and everybody's new some time), you'll want to know all about us!

SCHEDULE FOR ALL FRESHMEN *

| | |
|---|---|
| 7:30 A.M. | First Bell |
| 8:00 | Breakfast |
| 8:45 | First Period |
| 9:45 | Second Period |
| 10:45 | Third Period |
| 11:45 | Milk and Crackers |
| 12:00 | Activity |
| 1:00 | Lunch |
| 1:45 | Fourth Period |
| 2:45 | Fifth Period |
| 3:45 | Gym |
| 5:00 | Study Hall |
| 6:00 | Vespers |
| 7:00 | Dinner |
| 7:30 | Free Period |
| 8:00 | Study Hall |
| 10:00 | Free Period |
| 10:30 | Lights-Out |

* Any student who wishes to request a change in her schedule, for health or other reasons, should report to Miss Abloi's office at 1:00 P.M., Tuesday, October 2.

I had just finished reading that page on my way back up to the room when Miss Pick shot around a corner.

"Got your pamphlet, Rachel, I see," she said approvingly, stopping on a dime in front of me.

"Yes, ma'am. I was just thinking about requesting a change."

"You needn't say 'ma'am.' 'Miss Pick' will do nicely. No unreported health problems, I trust?"

At that moment I was about to tell her I had had polio as a child and could not walk to so many classes, but I decided, since it was a complete lie it might cause me difficulty later on.

"No," I said. "But this doesn't allow me any time to play."

"Play?" she asked. "Play what?"

"The piano. You remember, I'm going to be a concert pianist when I grow up," I explained. "I think I mentioned that when you interviewed me."

"Oh, of course!" said Miss Pick, smiling once again. "We love to see talent blooming in our girls, but I'm very much afraid we cannot change your schedule except for reasons of health."

I was sorry I had not mentioned the polio story. "But it says right here, 'health or other reasons,'" I insisted.

"Rachel," said Miss Pick, putting her hand on my shoulder and holding it tight. "You are going to have to learn that exceptions cannot always be made for you." Here she looked for a reaction, but I clammed up. "But I do have an idea," she said brightly. "We're putting on the *Mikado* for our school play this Christmas. You can choose that as the activity for your activity period. Then you can play a whole extra hour a day."

"The *Mikado!* But I hate Gilbert and Sullivan!" (I could have dropped a hot brick on her foot.)

"You hate Gilbert and *Sullivan!*"

"No, I don't mean that I actually hate Gilbert and Sullivan. It's just that my teacher at home wants me to play Mozart and Bach."

"But this is what the North Place music department suggests," said Miss Pick smoothly. "Naturally you may continue your lessons on Saturdays, if you wish, but we do encourage our girls to participate with others in whatever they like to do. For instance, if you want to write, there's the school paper. We have ballet and an art show and perhaps, if you'd like to, Rachel, you could give a recital for the school. Would you like to do that?"

"I don't know. I don't think I'm good enough yet," I stammered. "That's why I wanted to—"

"Rachel," she interrupted, "I'm sure you'll find wonderful new things opening up to you this year. Be patient. All the girls just love being in the Christmas musical. If you've never done anything like it before, you can't imagine the warmth and spirit that go into it. Wait till you meet Miss Howard, the piano teacher. You might even get to like Gilbert and Sullivan, too!"

She twinkled a smile and spun on her heel and was off.

"But the 'other reasons'!" I yelled down the hall after her, with my thumb on the sentence in the pamphlet.

"That's only for special cases!" she trilled back and vanished into a large oak doorway. I was too terrified to follow, but had I done so, I'm sure the door would have been locked behind her, as if it knew just who was allowed in and out of it.

I really must stop imagining things like that and scaring myself. I must concentrate on changing that schedule. I wonder who the special girls are, though? Probably very bright, very retarded, or black. In any case, I am evidently not special. I checked out the wallpaper once more on the way back to my room, making sure no one was looking. Whatever acid is in my fingers had no particular effect on it, but possibly it is long term. Rachel Saseekian's hand print may show up in fifty years and no one will know who did it.

Rock music was thumping and roaring out of practically every room on the corridor, mine included. When I peeked in there were five or six girls dancing to a screaming record. I turned to go away but Ebbie caught a glimpse of me out of the corner of her eye and shouted, "Hi, Rache, come join us. I got the new Grateful Dead album!"

Although I've practiced at home with a towel, it doesn't do very much good. I'm a terrible dancer and have no sense of timing. The worst of it is, everyone says, "But you're so musical. I don't understand, you're so musical!" So I envied those girls tremendously as they danced around the room. I've been over this at least fifteen times with the Choice Genie. (No, I will not give up the piano in order to learn to dance.)

"We'll teach you," said Ebbie, smiling. She must have read my thoughts.

"No thanks," I said. "Not now. I'm not feeling too well."

"Cramps, eh?" asked Ebbie, still dancing. "I have some pills if you want them."

THAT GIRL IS A WITCH!

"That's O.K.," I stammered, lying down on the bed and looking at the wall with great interest. (Now I'll have to spend the whole year living that down.)

Then I noticed the new poster. It was a blown-up photograph of a Hell's Angel on a motorcycle. He had a skull and crossbones on his T-shirt, black leather pants studded with chrome, and high boots. His crotch jutted forward impertinently astride a mammoth machine, but the face had been taken out and in its place was superimposed the face of Robert Kennedy.

I sat bolt upright and demanded, "Get that poster down! That's a sacrilege!"

The dancing and music stopped abruptly.

"A what?" asked one of the girls.

"A sacrilege! That's a disgusting poster!"

"But they're very rare," said Ebbie. "You can't get the Kennedy posters anymore."

"Take it down," I insisted. "Robert Kennedy was one of the greatest men who ever *lived!*" Some girl muttered something about radical leftists.

"O.K., all right," sighed Ebbie, climbing up and unhooking it. "If it matters that much to you, but just because he's dead doesn't make him great."

"You *like* Robert Kennedy?" asked another girl.

"My parents have his picture on the mantelpiece at home. John Kennedy's too," I announced to all of them.

"You're *kidding!*"

"Whose picture have your parents got? Nixon's? J. Edgar Hoover's?"

The girl observed that she didn't know anyone who had pictures of politicians in the house. Then they all moseyed out with their records. Ebbie stayed, fidgeting a bit and arranging things symetrically on her bureau top. I turned my face to the window, feeling angry and sorry all at once.

"It's O.K.," she whispered after a moment and

tried to pat me on the back. I jerked away from her. (There's something in the Bible about a person turning into a pillar of salt. I'm not exactly sure why they did, but I feel as if I'm doing just that when someone tries to touch me. I did like Ebbie better for trying, but when people pat me or put their arm around me, I feel obliged to do the same thing back. So I can't do anything but freeze.)

"Go away, please," I said to her, and she did, but not without a "Sorry for even being born!" For the next hour I tried to cry but couldn't and finally dozed off until the dinner bell.

Someone has just come into the lavatory. It must be about two o'clock in the morning. Whatever time it is, I've been writing so long my fingers are stiff.

I don't want to go to bed yet. Falling asleep is delightful, but waking up is awful, because there's no way of making this place go away. I fell into an extraordinary dream this evening before dinner. I found myself in a room full of beautiful unknown girls. I was in the corner of the room, wrapped up in brown paper like a carpet, leaning against the wall, afraid to sit down, or in any way show any bodily part of me. Robert Kennedy came in, smiling. "It's all right," he said, in a voice not his own, and he unwrapped me very slowly. No one in the room noticed, and I followed him out into the hallway. Suddenly, he was shot from behind. "I didn't do it, I didn't do it!" I yelled, but no words came out of my mouth and the thought of the words came slowly, like footsteps in a dream where you cannot run. A tiny red flower appeared on the back of his head, and I rushed to cover it with my hand and keep it from bleeding. "No good. No good," said a voice behind me, and I wept in the dream, as if someone I knew and loved very much had died.

It *is* two o'clock in the morning. I heard a church bell just now, somewhere out in the world. If I keep going here, I may become sleepy. Writing keeps the panic away. A doctor a day keeps the apples away. Gibberish.

The food is very good here. Much better than at the school cafeteria at home. Asparagus tonight. They must be horribly expensive, because they're out of season in September. Student body of 600 girls. Half a pack of asparagus each at 79¢ a package would come to about 40¢ per girl.

$$600$$
$$\times .40$$

$240.00 just for asparagus
$4000.00
$$-.40$$

$3999.60 left of my tuition because of asparagus

Dinner is held in Massey Hall, another very churchy place. There are stained-glass windows on both sides of the room and enormous dark brown beams holding up the roof. (I want to conduct some really dark brown music [Brahms] at this point.) I sat next to Ebbie, who was as bouncy and friendly as ever, although I know I'm not imagining her to have been extremely pissed off at me for telling her to go away in the middle of an affectionate gesture.

The names of the rest of the girls at the table were decidedly peculiar: Buffy, Mimi, Didi, Devvy (for Deverest she explained). I asked Ebbie what her name was short for.

"Eberhard," she gasped, rolling her eyes and mock upchucking.

"Sounds familiar," I said.

"Of course it sounds familiar. It's on practically every pencil in the country," she explained with a sigh.

"But I don't see why they named you that."

"Because they didn't have a boy," said Ebbie, stuffing a salad leaf into her mouth. I still didn't understand.

"Uhmp. Well," she said, "my father is Eberhard Faber III, and since I'm the fourth daughter in a row and they didn't want to take a chance on having any more girls, they had to pass the name down to me. It'll have to go to my son."

That whole thing reminds me of a joke with Linda. We had a dollar bet as to whether there really is a woman named Enna Jetticks. (There isn't. We looked it up in the phone book.)

"There's a Boris Godunov in the New York City

phone book," I said meekly. Drew a blank. Then a "Who's Boris Good Enough?" "He's a Russian opera," I explained and then added, "but Ebbie's a nice name. It certainly isn't as bad as John or Bill. Supposing your father's name had been Herbert."

"I like Rachel," said Ebbie decidedly. "I wish I were a Rachel. Are you Jewish?"

"Yes." (I lied but it might get me out of vesper service.)

"Gee," said one of the other girls, "that's neat. You're the fourth Jew in the school. You must be smart."

"Well, I wasn't born Jewish," I admitted. "I made a personal conversion."

"Why?" asked a whole chorus of them.

What could I say? "Because it's a very fine religion," of course.

The ceiling of Massey Hall is a sea of names, columns and columns of them, in gold German-looking script. I noticed after a moment that there were small gold crosses following some of the names.

"How come so many nuns went here?" I asked Ebbie, squinting up at the ceiling.

"Nuns?"

"Lady ministers?"

"Oh, the crosses. That means they've died."

"You mean they wait for you to die and then put a cross next to your name?"

"They don't *wait* for you to die," said Ebbie.

"But someday, in a hundred years or so, there'll be a cross next to every name."

"I guess there will be."

"That's awful!"

"What's awful about it? I think it's a lovely tradition," said another girl, and suddenly they were all looking at me as if I were wearing a moon suit. "One of the best things about North Place is the tradition," she added.

"Balls."

"*What?*"

(Of course, I didn't really dare say "balls." I wanted to, but only said something like "Yes, I know." The gutless wonder. I'm going to have to watch my language. It occurred to me they might have some old woman here who sits in a room with a basin of water and soap, her only duty being to clean out the mouths of people like me, in public of course.)

Someone gaveled for attention in the front of the hall. Peering through the heads, I could just make out Miss Abloi's stumpy form on the dais between the American and, I guess, the North Place flags. "There will be an orientation assembly in Knapp Hall at 7:45," she announced through a microphone, slanted down to accommodate her. There was mass groaning at this. "Followed by cocoa and singing." Then she raised a small metal object to her mouth, blew a couple of notes and said, "We Celebrate." The whole hall full of girls rose as one and burst into a sixteenth-century English chorale.

"We celebrate, We celebrate, thy unbounded feast!"

A hundred thousand voices, or so it seemed, rose steadily and completely filled the hall with music. It was quite lovely, and I knew I ought to be singing with them. A panic came over me, and the invisible hand swept me out of the room and down the first dark hallway I could find.

No more fuzzy gold wallpaper, only a cool blue, in the pattern of a Japanese woven screen. I stopped to steady myself and looked out a window. The girls were already trooping into another building. I felt deliciously far away, for I could see they were making a great deal of noise, and yet I could hear none of it. Above the regular window, in red-and-green leaded glass, were the words "In this halcyon rest," but the sun disappeared behind a cloud and I couldn't make out the end of the inscription.

After a bit, I opened one of the many oak doors and stepped into a very cozy little library filled with leather-bound books that I dared not touch. Chaucer,

Alexandre Dumas. I've heard of them all and respect them in a fearful sort of way, knowing I should read them. Tonight, for instance, having missed the assembly, I really ought to have tried a Dumas, but there on the shelf next to it was Alice, and she was such a good old friend I couldn't resist taking *Through the Looking Glass* and curling up on the sofa with it.

For the first time I tried earnestly to figure out Lewis Carroll's rules for the chess game at the beginning of the story. I must have fallen right asleep, for the next thing I knew, a husky voice asked, "What are you doing here?"

"I'm sorry!" I said with a little shriek and began brushing myself off as if I had been rolling in a mud puddle. A chunky little woman in a blue-serge suit was staring at me with her arms folded. She had heavy, Coke-bottle spectacles, short black hair, and a very raw-looking complexion. I disliked her instantly. Then I noticed a small cross around her neck, with a slanted gold crossbar running through the stem. A Russian cross? Armenian maybe? It seemed more sentimental than religious. "You missed the assembly," she observed and plopped herself down on the couch. I tried to edge my way out of the room.

"I'm sorry," I said again. "I didn't know there was one."

"Oh, come now," she piped, adjusting those glasses

and looking up at me practically cross-eyed, as if she could barely focus. "You must have heard the announcement at dinner. I'm Miss Block, by the way."

"How do you do, ma'am. I'm Rachel Saseekian. I must have missed the announcement."

Miss Block laughed in a little explosion. "Hee!" she said. "I'll tell you a secret. I missed it too. I stayed in my room and read. I couldn't bear the thought of all that cocoa and singing. Do you like singing?"

"Well, I like to listen," I said. "I'm really—I mean I have a terrible voice and I hate singing in groups."

"You do, eh? So do I," she said very definitely and took off her glasses and wiped them on her skirt.

"Yes. It always reminds me of camp."

"Camp, eh? What did they do to you in camp?"

I was truly astonished. Grown-ups usually don't put questions like that. She seemed to understand before I even explained. "Well," I told her, "they had these things they called 'sings.' Everyone had to gather around a campfire and put their arms around each other's shoulders and sing all the camp songs."

"Barbaric!" Miss Block puffed.

"Barbaric?"

"Forced camaraderie. Forced, forced, forced. That's why I didn't go tonight." Here she put her glasses back on and threw back her head, staring at me intently. "Forced!" she repeated.

"Did I do something wrong by not going?" I asked her, feeling on safe ground at last.

"Not at all. You don't mention me, I won't mention you. But if you get into any sort of trouble, just say you were talking to Miss Block."

"Thank you," I mumbled, and for the first time today I started to cry. "I didn't want to come to North Place at all," I said, ashamed and relieved all at once.

"I could see that the moment I came in," said Miss Block.

"How could you see that?"

"There are a few like you every year." She said. "They settle in after a while though. You will too."

"Oh, I don't think I will at all." I explained about the schedule.

"Oh, *you're* the pianist!"

"The pianist?"

"We've all heard about you, at least the interested teachers have. You're a public-school girl, right?"

It sounded so inferior and horrible. "Yes," I said.

"Good for you. We need a little fresh blood with all these socialites." Miss Block took *Through the Looking Glass* from the sofa. "An excellent thing to read," she said, and curled up exactly as I had on the couch. "And remember, if anyone asks you, you've been talking to Miss Block."

I turned for a second in the doorway. "Thank you, Miss Block. By the way . . ."

"Yes?"

"I did hear that announcement at dinner."

"I know."

I wandered out to the moat for a while before coming back to the dormitory. I suppose it's against the rules, but since it's my first night here I should be able to get away with it.

The water felt pleasant and warm on my feet, and the bulrushes hid me nicely. I felt so good I was able to hum one of John Dowland's Pavans in its entirety, without a mistake, as I gazed at the dark, monstrous building in the middle of the moat.

## Tuesday, October 2

This was the first day of classes, mostly a doling out of books. I have to take Latin but want French instead.

I appeared punctually at 1:00 at Miss Abloi's office for a schedule change. There were six girls waiting ahead of me, and by the time I got to see her I was sure I would try her patience with my request, but she sat across the desk from me looking as if she had nothing in the world to do but change schedules. I noticed the birthmark again and could picture my father explaining that that was the reason Miss Abloi never got married. Miss Abloi told me it was beyond her power to allow me more free time.

"Who would be able to do something?" I asked.

"Only Miss Pick, at special request," she said, hands folded.

"I've already asked her," I admitted, "but do you suppose if I agreed to play in the *Mikado*, she'll let me have another extra hour a day to practice?"

"Rachel, are you trying to strike a bargain?" Miss Abloi asked, shifting around in her dress.

I sat up very straight and told her I'd play a mean *Mikado* for them if they'd let me have another hour to practice.

"I beg your pardon!"

"Have you a score?" I asked. "If you have a score I'll run through it once, and then play it by heart."

"Score?" she asked.

"The music. I'll show you."

"I'm afraid it cannot be arranged," she said, looking at her watch. "Now is there anything else?"

"Well, there is one thing," I said, feeling I had made a very bad beginning. "I wanted to ask you if I could take French instead of Latin."

"Why, Rachel?"

"Well, ma'am, I just feel I'd like to."

"Latin is the basis of all Romance languages."

"Yes, I know. But I'd like to have four years of French. That way I'd really get to know the language."

"Well, you certainly can take French as well as Latin, if you like," she offered.

"Will that get me out of gym?"

"I'm afraid gym is required."

"Oh. Well, I'll think about the French then. Thank you, ma'am."

"One more thing, Rachel," said Miss Abloi, opening a drawer and fishing around in it. "I understand you've changed your religious affiliation." I blushed. "It's perfectly all right," she said. "Just change this line on your transcript, please."

I crossed out "Presbyterian" and wrote in "Jewish."

"In light of this," I said seriously, "I'd prefer not to attend vesper services."

"Rachel," said Miss Abloi.

"Yes, ma'am?"

"I think you spend entirely too much time wondering how to get out of things."

After dinner we had a free half hour, and I ran down to the little library again. There was Miss Block, sitting behind her Coke bottles and looking as if she expected me.

"Stupid!" she said, when I told her about the

changes I'd tried to make. "They are so stupid sometimes." Then she went to the window and lit a cigarette. "We're not even supposed to smoke in front of the students," she huffed. "Sets a bad example, they say. I'll do what I can about the Latin. I don't know if I can help you. In the meantime you'd better go to study hall and make as few waves as possible."

"Waves?"

"Trouble."

"Why should I trouble them by staying here in the library? I have no real homework anyway."

Miss Block sighed out a huge puff of smoke. "Believe me, they think it's trouble."

I was caught in study hall writing in my diary. Luckily I shut it in time to reveal only the spine, which of course says *Le Compte de Monte Cristo*.

"I beg your pardon," said the teacher. "Are you writing in that book?"

"It's mine," I said. "I'm taking notes."

"Aren't you a freshman?"

"Yes, ma'am."

"You needn't say 'ma'am.' My name is Miss Dowd. Are you taking French this year?"

"I hope to switch from Latin to French."

"Well that certainly is a difficult book to begin with," she said, shaking her head.

"My father is French," I explained.

Miss Dowd went away, saying that was very interesting.

There's an open window on the ground floor of my dormitory building, so it's fairly easy to sneak out to the moat. The night felt wonderfully cool after that hot stuffy hall. A half moon danced on the surface of the water, and I skipped stones for about an hour. Is that the real world out there at the moat? Or is it real here in the dorm? As long as I can go there every night, I think I'll manage. Ebbie hasn't said anything about my not being in the room at night. I've decided I need time away from everyone, not so much for the piano, but just to be by myself for a while.

## Wednesday, October 3

I'm in another lavatory, this time in the school infirmary. It must be four in the morning. I'm so sleepy, I think I'll write about this tomorrow.

## Thursday, October 4

Last night I fell asleep writing on the john. At the moment I'm still in the infirmary, in bed, and expected to be released and go to vespers in about two hours. They don't seem to care if I'm Jewish, but I might as well plug away at that one, since they'd never understand if I said I was nothing at all.

Yesterday afternoon was my first try at what they call field hockey, same as ice hockey but without the ice, and using a ball instead of a puck. After about three minutes on the field I got hit with the ball, right above the eye. Everyone crowded around.

"I'm just fine, really, I'm just fine," I insisted. I prayed my eye would swell up and get nice and ugly, which it obligingly did by the end of the period. Gamely, I continued to try and play hockey, luxuriating in sudden dizzinesses. Everyone kept asking me if I was sure I was all right. In the end I keeled over. It was a combination real faint and wishful-thinking swoon. I was on the ground, my eyes were closed, and I must have looked really awful. I decided not to allow them to carry me from the playing field—that would be overdoing it—but I did let a couple of them help me up. Ebbie Faber was assigned to take me to the infirmary, since she had apparently spent one summer working as a nurses' aide.

"I don't want to go to the infirmary," I told Ebbie. "Let's go back to the room."

"Why don't you want to go to the infirmary?" she asked. "It's neat. You get to miss vespers, and classes, and everything."

For a second I considered my position. Daddy has taught me to play poker, and sometimes the best thing to do if you're holding good cards is to wait and not bet too heavily at first. "I won't go to any hospital," I said. "I'm perfectly all right. You wait, when I just clean my eye off it'll be fine."

"O.K.," Ebbie agreed reluctantly, "but don't blame me if you get into trouble."

Miss Abloi conducted me personally to the infirmary when, after fifteen minutes of vespers, I fainted. This time it was a real faint. She took my arm and walked very slowly, meanwhile telling me about her sister Ruth in Minneapolis.

Apparently her sister was a very bright girl, musically talented like me. She had joined a convent when she was nineteen but after two years had decided the life was not for her and so discarded the veil and attempted to make a new beginning on the outside. That didn't really suit her either, and so she was never happy, in or out of the convent. Miss Abloi added that they were not a Catholic family and that Ruth had made her own conversion, like Luci Baines Johnson a few years back. I said that it was too bad about Ruth, expecting a parallel to be drawn to me, but she continued about her brother, who had passed away a year ago last April.

"Died under the knife," said Miss Abloi.

"You mean he was mugged?" I asked, hoping for gory details.

"You wouldn't say that," Miss Abloi sighed. "It was the doctors."

"Doctors?"

"An operation. They said it was a brain tumor."

"I'm very sorry to hear that."

"Not that doctors aren't necessary," she went on, as if I had attacked the medical profession. "When you need 'em, you need 'em."

We had reached the infirmary by this time. I began to think about concussions and brain damage.

The infirmary lobby looked just like the rest of the school. It didn't even smell medical. There were identical groups of tables and straight-backed chairs along the walls, and the same silver bowls filled with green-and-gold straw flowers. There was also a very large oil painting of an old woman above the reception desk. I asked Miss Abloi who it was. She didn't appear to notice my question but punched impatiently on a small, silent bell. It must have rung somewhere, because a young woman came bounding out, adjusting a nurse's cap. "Miss Meloncherry will be right with you," she said and gave me three carbon forms to fill out and left.

"Miss Bennett," said Miss Abloi.

"Excuse me?" I asked.

"Our founder." Miss Abloi pointed to the picture of the old lady. Her face looked a bit like the Pekingese she was holding. In the background were the usual wisps and floatings you find in portraits of old ladies.

"Died at the age of ninety-two," said Miss Abloi.

"I hope she didn't suffer much," I said, trying to be positive.

"Suffer?"

"Well, under the knife, you know," was all I could think to say.

"Miss Bennett was never under the knife."

A nurse appeared from around a corner. "Rachel!" she said. I coughed. They all seem to know me here.

They put me in a room with another girl, soundly sleeping behind a waist-high screen. They gave me a glass of water in a cup stamped:

PATIENT:

ROOM:

DOCTOR:

(DENTURE CUP)

About an hour passed. "Dear God," I prayed, ashamed of myself for wasting prayers. "Please don't let the swelling go down. Please let me be sent home to Brooklyn tonight." I hopped out of bed every once in a while to check it in the mirror. A lovely blue lump had risen and showed no signs of going away. I had not used the ice bag the nurse had placed by the bed, but it did give me the idea of putting hot water on the eye instead. If cold is good, hot will be bad, I reasoned. Unfortunately, the hot water didn't seem to make it look any angrier or bigger. Meanwhile, the girl in the other bed hadn't moved an eyelash.

Eventually Miss Meloncherry reappeared. "Doctor's here," she whispered and helped me out of bed by the armpits.

Miss Meloncherry took me into the examining room. She began to finger instruments and close drawers. The doctor was comfortable and Henry Fonda-like and seemed to understand right away when I gave a meaningful glance in her direction. "Uh, that will be fine, Miss Meloncherry," he said. She stopped cleaning the rubber floor pedal of the examining table and left promptly.

Over the past few days I've been going in and out of lying moods, and not trusting much of anyone. But I so liked Doctor Henry Fonda that I just broke down and wept. I told him there was probably nothing the matter with my eye, but that I hated North Place and wanted to go home, and couldn't he do something for me, coming from the outside world as he did.

"The outside world?" he asked.

"Well, the free world then," I said, blowing my nose on his handkerchief.

"The free world?" he repeated.

"The other thing is," I told him, "I think they have some sort of file on me here. Everyone seems to know something about me I haven't yet told them."

"They do, eh?"

"I'm turning into a different sort of person than I was before."

"Different?" he asked. "Tell me more."

"I want my mother and father!" (Why did I have to say that?)

"Of course you do, Roberta."

"Rachel."

"Rachel. Tell me, Rachel, how long have you been feeling that you're living outside the free world. That people are after you with secret files, so to speak."

"I didn't mean it that way. I mean not like Russia or anything. You think I'm crazy!"

"Rachel, I don't think you're crazy, but you did tell me those things in your own words. Has this feeling come about since you were hit this afternoon?"

"I don't know. I don't know. I just want to go home. I have a wonderful doctor at home, and I'm sure my mother would rather—"

"I'm sure too, Rachel," he said, "but we don't want to alarm your parents, now do we?"

"I know they'd want to know if I was hurt."

"Of course they would. Of course they would, but they'd also want to know, from a doctor, the extent of the injury. Otherwise they'd be upset."

"I guess so." I sobbed.

"I promise you," he said, getting his stethoscope out of his bag, "that we'll give them a call the minute we know. O.K., pumpkin?"

"What are you going to do with that?"

"Deep breath."

"But it's not my heart, it's my eye!"

"Never mind, now I'm just going to look at your eye—"

"Don't *touch* it! It hurts. I know I'm a sissy but—"

"I promise not to touch it; I'm just going to look at it. Look to your right, now left. How long have you had these feelings about Communists chasing you?"

"Communists!"

"Well, you mentioned the free world and the Russians."

"But you don't understand. I meant that as a—"

"Have you been harboring these feelings for a long time?"

"I never had those feelings before!"

"Just since you were hit in the head, right?"

"No. I mean yes. Now you think I have brain damage!"

"Rachel, I never said anything like that." He folded

up his stethoscope. "We're just going down to the hospital for a little X ray."

"A *little* X ray!"

"O.K., a big X ray then." He chuckled.

"A *big* X ray! You can get cancer from too many X rays!"

"Rachel, I promise you, you won't get cancer."

"I want to call my parents!" I said.

"You don't want to worry them now," he said again in the most wonderful voice.

"No, but please let me call." I remember hugging him close to me and crying uncontrollably. I didn't care at that point if I had brain damage for the rest of my life. I just wanted to go home.

"Now, we can't have too much of that," he said.

"I wasn't making a sexual advance, if that's what you think!" (*Why* did I say *THAT?*)

"Of course you weren't, but you have a lot of worries—Communists, secret files, cancer, sexual advances," said Doctor Henry Fonda.

I decided to go meekly and not say anything else for fear of putting more ideas in his head.

I sat in the back seat of the doctor's car with Miss Abloi, who had undoubtedly come along to make sure I didn't escape. The gates of North Place disappeared behind me, and I felt a weight lift from my head. I even kidded myself that I would never see the school again. The doctor put on the radio. I asked him to please change the station, since it was playing the *Theme from Love Story*. He did so, with a little knowing glance at Miss Abloi.

The X rays showed nothing, and I didn't dare ask again for permission to call my parents. Miss Abloi didn't say a word during the ride home from the hospital. I had the impression she was disappointed in me for not having a concussion. The doctor also switched the radio station back. This time Mantovani was playing "The Impossible Dream." It was only nine o'clock, but they put me to bed anyway. Miss Meloncherry gave me a pill, which she said was "nothing but aspirin." It looked awfully colorful for an aspirin, so I kept it in my gum until she left the room.

The moment I spat out the pill, my roommate sat bolt upright in bed. "Hi!" she said. "What're you in for? Oh, my, look at your eye!"

Her name was Carlisle Daggett. She was fat, with a bad complexion, and had messy, curly hair. In short, she looked not at all like any of the other North Place girls. She wanted very much to get out of the infirmary, she told me as she ripped off her nightgown and pulled on a tentlike dress. I liked her instantly.

"They send me in here every three weeks or so for allergies," Carlisle said. "I don't have any allergies, but the minute you sneeze in this place, they come running up with enema bags."

"Enema bags!" I winced.

"Oh, Meloncherry's big on purging the system," Carlisle said. "She's a hundred and forty-seven years old, so maybe's she got a point. Are you coming?"

"Are you kidding?" I asked her.

She smiled a foxy smile at me. "Of course not. Look, we can get out easily. It's on the ground floor, and there's a window in the bathroom. They never check on you once they think you're asleep."

"Yes, but they'll check to make sure I *am* asleep first."

Carlisle pointed to the pill I had spat out. "That," she said dramatically, "is a left hook."

"A left hook?"

"Like if Muhammed Ali hit you in the puss. They've been giving them to me every night. But tonight I didn't swallow it. They won't check. Meloncherry falls asleep at nine thirty, and the other nurse never leaves her solitaire game."

"But it's against the rules," I pleaded. "I've broken so many already; they'll do something horrible to me."

"Rules, schmules."

It was so nice to hear a "public schoolism" as Mother would say, and I was so miserable at being still at North Place that I decided to go.

"Live dangerously," Carlisle whispered as we crept out the bathroom window. She was incredibly agile for one so plump. I was terrified of being caught, but no one saw us, and we dashed out of the school grounds through the woods.

I felt for a moment that I was a little kid again back home, playing a game of cowboys and Indians, a pack of shrieking children after me, all to result in a huge wrestling match on the ground. But the only sounds were an old hoot owl and the rustling of leaves and twigs beneath our feet.

It took forty minutes to get into Boston by streetcar. The few places that seemed open in the city were the bus station and some bars. Carlisle claimed to have been in most of the bars. "Isn't that against the rules?" I asked.

"Of course." She chuckled and said it was part of the reason she had been made a "special."

We decided on the bus-station coffee shop. I refused to go into a bar, not so much because the school prohibits it, but because Mother and Dad would have a fit. I asked Carlisle what "special" meant.

"Well, it depends," she said, pouring at least ten spoons of sugar into her coffee. "We live in Quordoset Hall—"

"The one with the moat?" I asked.

"That's it. We go to classes just like you, and it's

all part of the same school, but we never get to see you except in the infirmary or by accident."

"Why?"

"Because we're all social problems or mental problems or something that doesn't fit in. There are twelve absolute geniuses, fourteen backward girls, and about twenty like me. I was transferred from the regular school last year. My parents have enough money to keep giving the school enormous grants, and they want me away from home. They also want me to get through North Place and go to Wellesley or something." The last she said with a sneer and a knowing look at me.

"What's Wellesley?" I asked.

"Wellesley is *it!*" she snorted in surprise. "Wellesley is where my old lady went, and, man, Wellesley is *it*. It's where every square wants to go to college. It's just like this hole except they give you a little more freedom."

"Well where *do* you want to go to college?" I asked.

"College! Man, college is a bad scene. I don't want to go to any college and get some pissy degree and marry some creep from Harvard."

"But how are you going to succeed in life if you don't go to college?" I asked.

"SUCCEED IN LIFE!" She opened her mouth into a positive parallelogram. "How old are you anyway?"

"Thirteen," I said miserably.

"Oh, Christ. I'm sorry."

"Sorry for what?"

"I'm seventeen, a junior," she said.

"Is being special awful?" I asked.

"Not so bad. You get to see a shrink twice a day if you want, but I'm fed up."

"What's a shrink?"

"Head shrinker. A psychiatrist. That's for the sickies like me, of course. The geniuses only do it if they want to, and the cretins they don't bother with."

"Cretins?"

"Poor little rich girls. They can't compete in the regular school, but they're rich as shit and wind up at junior colleges. They're not allowed to apply to four-year places unless it's somewhere in the South. We have the daughter of Westinghouse, the daughter of General Tires, and the daughter of Air France."

"I'm rooming with the daughter of Eberhard Faber pencils," I observed.

"Ebbie Faber?"

"Yup."

"Watch out for her."

"Why?"

"Ebbie's on Honor Court. She'll turn you in as quick as talk to you. She's dumb as they come too, been a freshman three years."

"Why don't they make her a special then?"

"They wouldn't dare. Besides, Ebbie loves it. Perpetual youth."

I wanted to know why Carlisle had been made a special. She ordered another cup of coffee and began telling me a long story, beginning with her parents. She said they were a million miles away from where she was. "Don't you feel that way too?" she asked.

"Sometimes," I allowed, "but not all the time."

"Well, with me it's all the time," she said. "The last time I got kicked out of boarding school they sent me to a reform school for four days to teach me a lesson."

"A *reform* school! I don't believe it. That's where they send orphans and street killers and stuff." I looked at Carlisle's face, but she didn't seem to be lying.

"You better believe it," she insisted. "Old Robert A. Daggett don't mess around. He let them send me up to a place in northern Massachusetts. Just four days, of course, just a warning, but next time he'll do it for keeps. He laughed at me afterward and told me that was just a taste of what would happen if I ever tried to run away again."

"But *no* parents— I mean I've never heard of anything like that in my whole life."

"Baby, baby, baby," said Carlisle, shaking her head and biting her lower lip. "You don't *know*. You're just thirteen years old and maybe I shouldn't be telling you this kind of thing, but you'll learn anyway. Maybe most parents wouldn't do a thing like that, but mine did. Holy shit, I could tell you stories—"

"I wish you wouldn't use words like 'pissy' and 'shit' and things like that," I said angrily.

"JESUS!"

"Jesus, what?"

"Man, if there's one thing you'll learn in this place it's how to swear!"

"Is that what they made you a special for?" I asked impatiently.

She laughed a bit at this. "I've been very patronizing, and I'm sorry. If there's one thing I can't stand it's people being patronizing. Also I won't swear if you don't like it."

"I say 'balls' sometimes," I admitted.

"So do I," said Carlisle, and she smiled at me. Then she offered me a cigarette. I figure there has to be a first time for everything, so I took it, knowing it was terribly against the school rules and dredging up a memory of a Norman Rockwell painting depicting a couple of boys trying out cigars and turning green behind the old barn door.

The cigarette made me feel high when I inhaled it. Everything started happening in the front of my mind, right between my eyes. "Is this a regular cigarette?" I asked.

"Once hundred per cent tobacco," she said, "You'll

feel funny if it's your first cigarette though."

"You still didn't tell me what you did that was so horrible," I said.

Carlisle tapped her cigarette expertly on her wristwatch. "Well," she began again, "I started running around and smoking dope the first year. Then I had a boy in my room and they caught me, and then there was the time when I ran naked in front of the Pinkies."

"Pinkies?"

"Yeah, those Pinkerton guards who patrol the whole school. Let me tell you about it. I had this really neat textbook in biology, the first neat textbook I've ever seen. It had about ten pages made of clear plastic, all printed with organs and bones and blood of the human body so that when you put them on top of each other you could see the whole scene, or you could see each system, muscles and stuff, by itself. Well, I decided to do it on myself, you know? I took all the right-colored oil paints and painted everything on the right place—stomach, ovaries, the works. Then I went and showed everyone on my corridor. They thought it was so great they brought me down to the corridor below, stark naked, organs and all, and then we ran into a Pinkie making his rounds. It was after lights-out, and he reported me for exposure or something. Got into a mess of trouble. My old man bailed me out though."

"Oil paint!"

"Yeah," said Carlisle. "It was a bitch getting it off afterward. Turpentine! But that's not why they finally threw me in."

"Why then?" I realized I was staring bug-eyed at Carlisle.

"You wouldn't believe it. I guess it was the straw that broke old Pick's back. We were supposed to memorize a poem in English class and give it, you know, in front of the class. Well, everybody took Rossetti or Shakespeare or Ferlinghetti or someone. One girl even got away with Rod McKuen. Can you imagine?"

"I don't believe it," I said, making a mental note to find out who he was.

"Well, anyhoo, I memorized a three-line poem and screwed it up." She looked up and smiled mischievously at me.

*The fog comes on little pig feet.*
*It sits quietly casing the harbor*
*And then splits.*

I began to laugh uproariously.

"Do you know the original, then?" Carlisle asked, surprised.

"Of course! Carl Sandburg. It's one of my favorite poems, but I think I like it your way better."

Carlisle stared at her coffee. "Gee," she said. "You're *fantastic*! No one I know knows it, or even gets it. Do you read a lot?"

"An awful lot. I love to read. Also, I love to play the piano."

"You'll do well here," she sighed. "You'll probably be an honor student. You're so straight."

"Straight?"

"Innocent."

"I'm afraid of being kicked out."

"What on earth for?"

I told Carlisle about the nightly visits to the moat, about wanting to change Latin to French, about skipping the assembly, asking for more time to play the piano, and generally not getting along with anyone.

"Well, hell," she said. "You said you have understanding parents. Why don't you just drop out, or wait till they kick you out, and go to another school where it isn't so rough?"

"Because my parents spent four thousand dollars on this place. They can't afford it, and I know I'll fail them if I don't make it."

"Make it? Make what?"

"I have to get through," I said with a sigh. "I have to get a good education and get into college and make friends. I mean, my parents didn't have anything. My father sweated all his life, and they've been saving up for years to send me here. They want me to have better than they did—and I guess I really love them very much, and anyway I want to do what's right. I don't want to be a coward and let them down."

Carlisle spent about a minute just tapping her finger-nail against her coffee cup before she answered me. I couldn't say another word for fear of breaking down and crying. I'm beginning to think I'm the world's biggest baby.

"Well, you gotta do it their way," she said at last. "If you want to stay here, you can't break too many rules or ask for privacy and stuff. They'll be lenient in the beginning, but they'll expect you to settle down after a while, and then they'll start socking it to you. Maybe you can ask your folks to let you transfer to another school."

"But I'd have the same problems."

"They're not all as bad as this one," she said. "North Place is a college mill. Practically everybody goes to Wellesley or Vassar and everybody is a good little girl. Do you want to be a good little girl for four years?"

"I guess I could do without dope and boys in my room," I said.

"You'll have to do without a lot more than that. Your folks can't pay off the school, like mine. Why don't you just go to public school? Public school is fun, boys in your classes, no dormitories, no milk and crackers at eleven o'clock."

"Mother would die."

"Mother, schmother," said Carlisle. "The thing of it is, do you think your mother is right?"

"Well, I don't know. I'm afraid, I guess. I'm afraid she may be right even though I don't really think she is. Oh *damn*."

"Why don't you come with me?" asked Carlisle.

"Come with you? Where are you going?"

"New York. Next bus, which should be in about fifteen minutes. The Village. I have some friends down there who'll take care of me. If they don't I can look after myself anyway, *by* myself. I'd take care of you though." She looked up. "If it's boys you're worried about, forget it," she said. "There's three girls, not counting me, and only two boys, most of the time, and one of the girls is over twenty. No one'll touch you if you don't want them to."

"No," I said, "I'm not worried about boys," but I admitted to her I hadn't had much contact with them.

Carlisle nodded quickly and said that she hadn't either when she was my age. "I didn't even have my period when I was thirteen," she said.

"You didn't?" I asked.

"Don't worry." She laughed. "No one likes to admit things like that, but pretty soon you'll be all right. You look pretty normal to me."

I must have turned scarlet, because she changed the subject. "Here," she said, writing something on the inside of a cigarette pack. "Here's my address, just in case you change your mind."

"I don't think I'll be coming," I said. "I'm afraid it would be a terrible mistake."

"Terrible mistakes all depend on how things come out," Carlisle observed. "For me, it would be a terrible mistake to stay here."

"Are you going to take dope and stuff and, you know, boys and everything?" I asked.

"Man," she said, "I'm going to be so straight, no one would know me. People who turn on all the time are messed up and unhappy. I'm messed up and unhappy here, and I feel like blowing my mind all the time, but I'm going to unmess myself."

"But I thought people who ran away to Greenwich Village all were kind of dope addicts and sex fiends and things."

"Not me. Not these people. We're all going to buy a farm in Vermont. You should meet them. You'd really love them. They're beautiful."

The man came and mopped up our table. "Closing time," he said.

"Bus for New York and points south," piped the loudspeaker, "loading now at gate one. Bus for Chicago, gate seven. Washington, Charleston, Miami, gate six."

"We'd better go," I said.

"How about Miami?" Carlisle asked. "Would you come if we went to Miami? Believe me it beats the great city of Boston."

"Why do you need me?" I asked, but Carlisle had

turned and was gathering up her stuff and didn't answer. "Won't you want a coat?" I asked.

"That's what I need a little kid like you for." She chuckled, looking away from me. "You're the type that remembers coats and thermos bottles."

"I guess it's my mother," I said apologetically. "She always worries about things like that, coats and thermos bottles and apples in the lunchbox."

"Well, mine never did," snapped Carlisle. "All my mother ever put in a thermos bottle was a martini."

"I'm sorry," I said, gazing straight at my feet as we walked toward gate one.

There was only one old woman waiting there for the bus. She had dreamy eyes and a coat of red-and-black spangly material that made me stare and go off into a dream.

"Would you?" said Carlisle suddenly, and she grabbed my hand and held it very tightly for a moment, biting back tears. "Are you sure you won't come?"

"I'm sure, but what about you? You don't look so sure."

"I'm sure all right. I'm just worried, that's all. This time it's for keeps. They won't pay to let me back again, and if I'm caught they'll send me to the funny farm."

"Well, you don't want some little kid along to get in the way," I said. (I think I remember that from a gangster movie.)

"You're right!" said Carlisle with sudden resolution, handing me the pack of cigarettes. "But come and see me sometime, and if you ever . . ."

"I know."

"And you won't tell."

"Swear to God and hope to die!"

"Well, I certainly believe that," she said, laughing. "You're honest, young but honest! *Ciao!*" And she tripped lightly up the steps of the bus.

I hid the pack of cigarettes quickly in my pocketbook. The North Place rule book says it is forbidden to smoke at any time, even during a vacation, and I wanted to take no chances. The bus pulled out, and I wished a little that I had been on it. I could have taken the subway from Forty-second Street and been home in an hour, but knowing I can do that anytime I want makes me feel better. I felt a surge of confidence and walked back to the streetcar.

## Friday, October 5

Classes all day today. Eye went down completely. Feelings of great fear are easing with the routine, but once in a while I look around and see strange faces, and panic overcomes me, I tried to call my parents last night, but they were out. In order to make a phone call, you have to fill out a slip with the person's name you're calling on it. The only telephone booths are in Miss Abloi's outer office, and although it seems quite private, Ebbie says there's a listening line, and the reason they make such a big deal out of phone calls is so that you don't call boys all the time. Wish I had one to call.

Ebbie is still a puzzlement. She is president of the freshman class, and a member of Honor Court. She's been a freshman two years in a row, not three as Carlisle said, but it doesn't seem to bother her in the least. She's fifteen years old and has been at North Place since the fifth grade.

We have kind of a truce between us now. She spends most of her time dancing in Devvy's room with her friends. I know they think I'm awfully strange for not liking dancing and records and talking about boys. Ebbie's boyfriend, Jack, is a senior at New England Military Academy. She asked me if I'd like to have a blind date with Jack's roommate for the Fall Prom. I told her my boyfriend at home wouldn't like it.

"Your boyfriend! What's his name?" she asked right off.

"Pete," I said falteringly. (If it comes up again I can always say we broke up.)

"I have an idea," she said. "Why don't you surprise him when you get home? I'll teach you how to dance!"

A trap. I had not exactly mentioned that I didn't know how. The girl is a mind reader. She put a record on the phonograph. "Here," she said, beginning to rock and sway with the music. "This is the basic motion."

"The basic motion?" I asked, sitting down on the bed.

"Yeah. I mean, if you can do this you can do anything, just improvise your own steps."

"But I don't want to."

"Of course you do. I mean you will, once you know how. Now stand up and give it a try. Don't be embarrassed!"

"I am embarrassed."

"Nonsense! How can you be embarrassed in front of me?" So I got up and tried to imitate what Ebbie was doing.

"Loosen up! Loosen up!" She laughed. "Now that's better. Put your hips into it!" (Ebbie's hips have to be at least thirty-five inches around. Mine are twenty-nine.)

"I'm sorry," I said, "I can't."

"Of course you can. Anybody can. Now don't give up so soon. Listen to the music and get the feel of what it wants you to do. There's nothing to it once you get the feel."

"But I don't understand music like this."

"You don't understand?"

"No. I don't like—I mean I don't listen much to popular music."

"But this is the Beatles!"

"That's popular music."

"But it's the *Beatles*!"

"I *know* it's the Beatles."

"Well, how are you ever going to have dates and go to dances and stuff if you don't even *try*?"

"I don't *know*!"

"Oh, for crissakes don't *cry* like that all the time!"

I hadn't even realized I was. I just wanted to get out of the room, but Ebbie was blocking the door and I couldn't.

"I only meant it for your own good," she said in a softer voice and turned the music off.

"Now you sound like a mother," I said. (The first good reply ever to Ebbie.)

"I'm sorry. I'm really sorry, Rachel." She tried to put her arm around me, but I pulled away, the pillar of salt again. Catching all the tears in my throat and swallowing them, I asked her, "Ebbie, isn't there anything that you really love to do? Something that means the world to you?"

"You mean Jack?" she asked.

"No, no, no, some*thing*."

"You mean like ecology or Women's Lib?"

"Not like Women's Lib!"

"Like what, then?"

"Like real music is for me. Like the piano is for me."

"But you're talented!"

"So what? It doesn't have to be the piano."

"But just because you play the piano doesn't mean you can't go out on dates and like the Beatles," she insisted.

"I never said it did."

"But that's what you mean, isn't it?"

"I'm just saying that I don't like that kind of music. Not that I don't like boys!"

"But how are you going to meet boys if you don't go to dances?" she asked. "The only way we can meet boys here is at the dances they have."

"At home we have boys in school," I explained. "You don't have to go to dances to meet them. You know them. You just know them like you know your friends."

"But you're not *at* home anymore. You're here. You don't *go* to that other school. I just don't know what else to say. I guess I'd better go." She sighed, throwing her hands in the air. "But don't say I didn't try."

"Don't say you didn't *try?*"

"If you must know," Ebbie said, "every new girl is assigned an old girl as a roommate. We're supposed to make you feel at home and see that you aren't lonely and stuff. And see that you aren't excluded. I felt I was making you feel excluded because I spend so much time in Devvy's room, dancing and stuff with all the kids. So I tried to teach you. All right?"

"Thanks, but I'd really rather read."

"Boy, are you an iceberg!"

"Ebbie, I think maybe you should change roommates or something."

"I think maybe *you* ought to change roommates!" she yelled.

"I just thought you'd be happier."

"I think maybe you'd be happier with no roommate at all!"

"Can I do that?" I asked, not angry anymore.

"Boy, you sure want the whole world to jump for you, don't you?"

"What do you mean by that?"

"You want to change Latin to French. You want extra time to play the piano. You want to room alone. Next thing you'll want maid service at the door!"

"How did you know about those other things?"

"I know because I'm on Honor Court," she said, turning red.

"Well, if you know so much, how come I can't have a room by myself?"

"Because you can't!"

"But why?"

"Because it's against the rules, that's why. If everyone wanted a room of their own, the school would have to be twice as big!"

"I have my own room at home. I do my homework and I don't stay up all night, and I have time to myself. Why can't I just have a little of that here?"

"Because you can't, that's why. Don't you think I

wish it were summertime, and I were out in Southhampton having a ball, too?"

"I don't want to be having a ball. All I want is a little privacy and freedom."

"Well, supposing everyone wanted that?"

"Well? What's wrong with that?"

"Maybe you ought to think twice about staying here, Rachel, if that's the way you feel," she said, walking out and slamming the door behind her. The argument had taken almost the whole half hour of free time. Lights-out bell rang, and I disappeared into the john where I am now writing. I'll go to the moat for a while before bed, but I'm getting sleepy so I guess I ought to close. The only other thing that happened today was that I was called out of history and had to report to Miss Abloi's office. She said a girl had disappeared out of the infirmary Wednesday night. Carlisle, of course. I told Miss Abloi I had seen nothing out of the ordinary.

*Saturday, October 6*

Saturday is the big day to go to town. You are allowed, however, only if you can get an upperclassman to go with you. That is difficult, since you have to know one. Ebbie seems to know all of them (another advantage of not being excluded, I have discovered), and she asked me if I'd like to go along.

"You mean I have to have someone accompany me if I want to go into town?"

"Of course, a senior or a junior."

"But Boston is so small. At home I'm allowed to go places in New York by myself."

Ebbie just sighed and tapped her foot. "I'm sorry for even asking," she said. "You go into New York City this afternoon, why don't you?"

"I have a piano lesson anyway," I said meekly.

"Oh, excuse *me*."

Miss Howard is a sweet old lady, but she is nuts on the romantic composers. I had to play Debussy and Chopin the whole hour. I must admit I played badly and quickly, but she didn't seem to notice and made no comment. I fumbled for excuses at the end of the lesson, trying to make it clear that I hated the pieces without hurting her feelings, but she only replied that she had sung the role of Yum Yum with the D'Oyly Carte in 1922 and did I think I would like to try out for the part?

I've got to get Mother and Dad to let me take private lessons in Boston.

Fifteen dollars a week?

$$9 \text{ months}$$
$$\times 4 \text{ weeks}$$
$$\overline{36} \text{ lessons (Make it thirty with vacations.)}$$

$$\$15$$
$$\times 30$$
$$\overline{\$450}$$

I could make that much this summer if Mother lets me work.

Afterward I played for two hours. I was furiously pounding out Mozart's Rondo in D Minor when Miss Pick suddenly appeared. After I don't know how much time, I noticed her standing behind the piano, beating time like a metronome.

"That was very lovely, Rachel," she said, when I had finished.

"Thank you," I answered a bit hesitantly. "It's not exactly what the teacher here wants me to play."

Miss Pick ignored this remark and looked right into my eyes. "Rachel," she said, "I want to have a talk with you."

"Certainly." I wished at that instant to apologize universally for everything I'd done wrong, all the rules I'd broken, and to promise that I would turn over a new leaf.

"Come into the library for a minute."

"Yes, ma'am."

"That's all right, you needn't say 'ma'am.'" Miss

Pick smiled and settled herself on a leather sofa. I sat opposite in a leather chair with my hands clasped tightly in my lap. "I understand you're not so happy with us," she began.

"Oh, I'm very happy, really, Miss Pick."

"Well, I have reason to believe otherwise," she said, examining her fingernails and smoothing her hands back and forth. I felt I'd better not ask why she had that impression, so I just said I was sorry and that I didn't want to be a troublemaker.

"Of course you don't. But you're talented. You're different from the rest of the girls."

I looked up momentarily into her gray-blue pools of eyes. There seemed to rest an understanding I had not seen before. "I'm sorry," I repeated, feeling enormously guilty for being such a prima donna.

"You needn't be sorry, Rachel. You come from a very different environment. I hope, though, that you like us and won't leave us."

God! I was mortified. I resolved immediately to adjust.

"I'm terribly sorry," I said again. "But it's just that when you're used to so much freedom and stuff, well, it's hard to change."

"Of course it is," Miss Pick nodded. "But we think very highly of you here at North Place. We think you're quite the most talented student we've had in a long time."

"Thank you," I answered, considering at the same time whether I should tell her that without more formal training I wouldn't amount to much, that I was quite an ordinary talent and that hundreds of kids my age and younger were being trained every day by professionals, and that if my mother weren't so afraid of hippies I'd be at Music and Art or Juilliard instead of here, but I didn't.

"Just hold on and give us a try," she said cheerily, squeezing my hand as she got up. "By the way, I hear you roomed with that Daggett girl Wednesday night."

"Daggett girl?"

"The one who's missing. She was in your room. But I imagine you were too sleepy to notice. Miss Meloncherry tells me you were given a large dose of sedatives."

"That girl! She didn't even move!" I mumbled.

"Is there anything you remember about her, Rachel?"

"Not a thing, ma'am."

"The 'ma'am' isn't necessary. You may—"

"Ma'am?"

"Yes, Rachel." She sighed.

"I'm sorry, Miss Pick. May I have permission to go into town and join Ebbie Faber shopping?"

"Of course. Go right ahead."


I stopped at a diner in the middle of Boston, ordered coffee, and took out a cigarette. There was something very cozy about sitting in a booth alone, with my coffee and my cigarette (second time ever!) reading *The Horse's Mouth*. Truck drivers and cab drivers and all manner of people drifted in and out, none of them particularly noticing me, every one coming and going of his own free will. It's odd how the normal little things, like being alone or meeting strangers, loom very large to me these days. I must have sounded like an idiot to the doctor Wednesday night, but I wouldn't take back anything I said. The real world just vanishes the minute I'm on school grounds, but he didn't understand. If I had awful parents, like Carlisle, I'd have run away too, changed my name, and never had anything to do with these people again.

Three girls from school came in, all upperclassmen whom I'd never seen before. They weren't in uniform, but I could tell they were North Place girls, just by the way they talked and laughed. Am I becoming a snob, the way Daddy said I might? How did I know they weren't just ordinary public-school girls? Is there a difference? I put out my cigarette immediately and left the diner while their backs were turned. Had they seen me alone and smoking they could have turned me in. I had to leave a whole dollar on the table without waiting for change. That leaves me just $12.00, enough for a one-way ticket home.

Is there something very unfeminine about sitting

alone in a diner booth reading? I put my hands over my ears just now, blocking another electric worry that has come from nowhere.

Tonight Ebbie and her friends asked me to go to the movies in Mattapequot with them. I am locking myself in a shell by refusing such things. *The Sound of Music* is playing and I didn't dare say what I thought of that. Besides, the night was soft and moonlit, and there was a whole apple orchard I hadn't explored behind the school.

"Are you just going to sit here and read?" asked Devvy.

"No, I think I'll take a walk tonight."

"Alone?"

"Yes, why?"

"It's against the rules."

"How can it be against the rules to walk in an apple orchard?"

"It just is. You might get raped."

"Well, that's the whole point of being out in the country, isn't it?" I asked. "We're miles from Boston. No one's going to rape me."

Devvy shrugged her shoulders. "You're going to get into trouble."

"Are you going to tell on me?"

"I never said I was going to tell on you."

"Well, how can I get into trouble then? They won't know I'm not at the movies."

"You have to sign out," she said. "You have to put down where you're going and who you're with and all that stuff."

"Well, I'll just sign out for the movies then."

Devvy got very upset. She grabbed me by the shoulders and shook me hard. "Listen," she whispered. "Some girl tried that last year. She signed out for a weekend home and went to a boy's college instead. The whole senior class almost didn't graduate because of her. Old Ice-pick told us last year that if anybody monkeys around with privileges, we're all gonna get it. She can take movies away from us."

"I didn't know that," I said. "But that's not fair. If one person does something, then everybody shouldn't—"

"Of course it isn't fair, but that's the way things are around here!"

"I won't sign out for the movies then."

"If you do," warned Devvy, "I'll have to go to Miss Pick." She put on her sweater to join the other girls, but stopped in the doorway, halfway out. "Look," she said. "I'm sorry. I've never told on anybody in my life. I won't say anything about your going out, not even to Ebbie."

"Not even to *Ebbie*!"

"Well, you know," said Devvy, twisting her thumbs around, and looking at a speck of dust on her shoe.

"I know?"

"Well, I mean Ebbie's a really nice girl and everything, but she's really straight about some things. She's the only freshman on Honor Court, and that's supposed to be a big deal."

"You mean she'd tell."

"She'd have to."

"She'd have to— What do you mean she'd *have* to?"

"Well, she couldn't lie about it if she knew."

"She could keep her mouth shut."

"But that defeats the whole purpose of the honor system," Devvy explained, shifting her feet uneasily and jamming her hands into her raincoat pockets. "People aren't supposed to lie. You're supposed to tell the whole truth without leaving anything out."

"And that includes telling on people."

"Yes, but if it's the truth you have to tell it."

I said nothing to that. Devvy began to look really uncomfortable. She itched her nose and fastened her buttons and went on, "If we didn't have the honor system, we'd have something worse. Didn't you hear Miss Abloi the first night?"

"I didn't go."

"You didn't *go*!"

"I was feeling sick."

"Oh. Well, anyway, she told about how the honor

system is a system of trust. She said how she knew people didn't like telling on each other, but that the school trusted them to do it, because it was more difficult to tell the greater truth or something. Anyway, the school trusts its students not to break the rules, and if they do, then they have to go and report it."

"Then what happens?"

"It depends on what you do. Usually you just get a couple of chits."

"Chits?"

"Demerits. Five and you're grounded for a weekend here. Twenty and you lose a weekend home. Like that. You can get out of them with Gettysburg Addresses, though. Five for one chit. I know a sophomore with nineteen chits. Every time she gets another she writes five Gettysburgs so she can go away for her weekends. One girl couldn't graduate last year because she still had fifteen chits at the end of the last term. Seventy-five Gettysburgs! She got all her friends to help her, but they recognized the different handwritings and gave her five more. She got 'em done though."

I was horrified. In one week I've amassed about a thousand Gettysburg Addresses. Ebbie knows I've been out of the room every night. She'll probably tell, too.

"Hey, why don't you come to the movies with us?" Devvy asked.

"Yeccchhhhh, *Sound of Music*," I said in my best public-school voice.

"Well, it's better than nothing."

"I think I'll stay, thanks."

"Oh, I forgot. You're talented, it's probably beneath you."

"Why do you hold that against me?" I asked, with my mouth full of those horrible tears, same as in interminable arguments with my parents.

"Nobody holds it against you." She shrugged. "You hold it against yourself. Every time someone tries to talk to you or get you to do something with them, it's like you shove a great big piano in between yourself and the other person. Maybe you're a real genius and that's how real geniuses act or something."

"Don't go," I said to Devvy suddenly.

"I have to. I'm going to be late; the others are waiting."

"Won't you go for a walk instead?"

"A *walk!*"

"Warm weather won't last much longer. It's so beautiful outside, and I haven't anyone to talk to."

"Robert Kennedy," said Devvy, screwing up her face.

"Robert Kennedy? What does he have to do with anything?"

"I never met anyone in my life who didn't hate Robert Kennedy," she continued thoughtfully. "And the first one who doesn't is a regular nut, but you just might be right, you know?"

I had no idea what she meant, but I tried something. "What do you think of the whole honor system thing, really?" I asked her.

"Frankly, I think it stinks, but it doesn't matter what I think—"

Ebbie appeared at the door. "Are you coming or what?" she asked.

Devvy looked around. "No," she said.

"You're not coming?"

"I've seen it three times, Eb, I can't hack it a fourth."

I thought perhaps Devvy would come with me, but she said she had studying to do, so I went alone. For the first time since I've been at North Place, I didn't enjoy being alone. I told myself I missed Swamp. Then I tried to hum some of my favorite music, but silly old tunes kept running through my head and I couldn't even do that. The orchard was windless, but the night had turned chilly and damp by the time I was able to sneak out. The moon had gone behind a cloud. I wandered in circles for a while with my hands in my blue-jean pockets against the cold, trying a bite out of an occasional apple, and feeling overall that things were slipping away. Something was very wrong inside. Not a matter of having no one to confide in, more not knowing what had actually gone wrong in the first place. What did Carlisle say? "Mother schmother." That's it. I'm afraid, I told Carlisle. You can keep thinking someone is wrong, as long as things are bearable, but if I keep breaking rules I'll be thrown out of here, and I'll never know whether Mother was right or wrong about people. My folks will have wasted their money on a cowardly, spoiled only child. I've got to "stick it out," as everyone keeps telling me.

When I reread what I have written in this diary, I feel ashamed of myself. I am a self-pitying person. I make everything sound as if the world is against me. Carlisle agreed with me though, but she has awful parents and a different outlook as a result. Something terrible is happening. If I had muscles inside my head, I'd stop it. I'm beginning to be a liar. I've never lied in my whole life, that I remember. I never wanted to. Why is it that lying here at North Place is different from lying at home? Maybe because I can't yet feel this a real place. Even the buildings and classes and food seem to be happening in someone else's life. It's like reading about Mexican children dancing around a stuffed paper rooster at Christmas time, and saying, "Oh, isn't that interesting the way they do things down in Mexico," or hearing about Chinese people doing calisthenics to a loudspeaker at five o'clock in the morning. It's part of some world very far away. But it doesn't make any sense to feel that way about North Place, because I'm here.

I crept in by the same downstairs window I've been using all week and went up to Devvy's room. She really was studying.

"You're really studying!"

Devvy turned around. She has a kindly face, despite a well-formed figure. She was lying on her bed, looking as if she very much enjoyed reading *Algebra in Our Lives*.

"The others," she said, rolling over, "most of 'em anyway, just cram before an exam. I'll give you a tip. If you study all the time, regularly, you'll never have to cram at all. You'll get A's all the time."

"I know. I study a great deal," I remarked, not catching her eye. Another lie. I'm not much of a student and am terrified I'll flunk out if I don't get kicked out. North Place is terribly difficult.

"That's good," she said cheerily.

"I thought everyone around here was smart," I ventured. "I figured most of the girls were A students."

"Nah! Look at Ebbie," said Devvy, waving her book. "She's been held back. She'll go to a junior college."

"I've heard of those."

"For the dumb ones." Devvy nodded conspiratorially. "I'm going to Radcliffe."

"Radcliffe?"

"Boy," she said, "if you're smart at all you better find out about Radcliffe."

"Why?"

"Because it's the best college in the world for girls! It's Harvard!"

"Gee, my father'd like that," I admitted.

"He's a Harvard grad?"

"He didn't go to college."

"He didn't go to *college*!"

"Self taught," I said, not mentioning the school of hard knocks.

That seemed to throw her for a moment. "What's your old man do?" she asked pleasantly.

I couldn't just say he was an electrician. "He's a writer, a novelist," I told her.

Devvy was very impressed. "What's his name? Saseekian? What's his first name?"

"I—I can't tell you."

"Who is he?"

"I said I can't tell you his real name."

"Why not?"

"I just can't."

"If you tell me, I'll tell you something you'll want to know."

"What?"

"I won't tell till you tell," Devvy said archly and began to read her Algebra text again.

"Tell me at least what it's about," I pleaded. "I might not want to know anyway."

Devvy digested this for a minute. "All right," she said. "You're in trouble."

"I'm in trouble? What for exactly?"

"I won't tell you another thing till you tell me who

your father is."

"Look," I said. "I won't tell unless you promise not to tell anyone else. He keeps his name a secret. Is it— is it leaving at night that I'm in trouble about?"

"Nope. Who's your father?"

"Norman Mailer."

"Norman *Mailer*!"

"Yup."

"You're lying!"

"O.K. If that's the way you want to look at it." I got up to leave.

"O.K.," she said. "All I can tell you is that you're in trouble about some girl who ran away from the infirmary last week. She was in your room or something. That's all I know."

My intestines tied themselves in a perfect square knot. "What girl?" I managed to say.

"I don't know. Some girl from the special school."

"How do you know all of this?"

"Ebbie—I heard her talking."

"But I didn't do anything!"

"Well, I guess you're not in trouble then."

Total fear! Can't read or concentrate. Came to the john to finish this. (Mother called today. They can't come see me tomorrow, but why don't I come home next weekend? YES!)

## Sunday, October 7

Church is required. The hymn singing was beautiful.
(Have I been missing something all these years of not
going to church? I love stained glass and organ music.)
Ah, well, if I couldn't bring myself to join the singing,
at least I said a small prayer for Carlisle.

This afternoon was "orientation tea" time at Miss
Pick's house. Her house is part of the campus—the
same gray-black stone, many carvings around the pointed
windows, and covered with ivy that looks as if it had
been planted over a hundred years ago. Inside, the rooms
resemble the library where I first found Miss Block.
Volumes and volumes, mostly leather bound. Dumas,
again, in French, Conrad, Dostoevski, complete sets of
books, not friendly looking at all.

There was a brown pastel of Miss Pick in younger
days above the mantelpiece. She was smiling and wearing a long gauzy gown in the portrait. Her hair was
braided around the top of her head like an old German
woman.

Miss Pick is not popular with anyone, I suppose.
None of the girls seemed to like the idea of going there,
but we all trooped in at last, and sat on the floor, since
the couches and chairs were filled with teachers. Sleepy
burr of conversation, tea pouring, cup clinking, thank

yous and no thank yous, and then I found Miss Block.

"How are you getting along?" she asked, grinning.

"Fine, thank you."

"Good. What are they teaching you in history?"

"About the Panama Canal."

"How interesting," she said, and we both laughed.

"Now that I've had my cup of tea," said Miss Block, gazing nearsightedly at the company, "I'm going to make my adieus, as they say, and go home and have a Scotch and a cigarette in peace. Drop in, if you like, on your way back."

I sat for a long time, stirring my tea idly and watching a man cut the grass far away on the playing fields. He drifted around in lazy circles, driving a giant wheat-sheaving sort of machine. Such a beautiful Indian summer afternoon. I could picture myself strolling out of the school grounds and down the long road beyond.

All of a sudden I was.

I don't remember quite how I got out of the house. I do recall going up to Miss Pick in a state of great agitation and interrupting a conversation very rudely.

"An old lady's just died," I stammered. "I'm sorry but I have to go to the funeral." Miss Pick looked at me uncomprehendingly.

Everything went black, but somehow I stumbled out of the house and ran until I was out of sight of the school grounds.

A police car came along and picked me up after about

half an hour. They desposited me back at Miss Pick's house. Terrified, I sat in a chair and watched while she thanked the police and fussed about for a few minutes, picking up after the departed guests.

"I understand, dear," she began, giving me a cup of hot black tea. "I just wish you wouldn't be so impulsive."

"You understand?"

"Yes, Rachel, I understand."

"Well," I said, groping for words, "I'm awfully sorry, Miss Pick. I didn't mean to run out, but I just couldn't bear it another minute."

She put her arm around my shoulders, but I withdrew. "Rachel, what couldn't you bear?" she asked. "We're all your friends here."

"I don't know." I was starting to sweat. "I just felt all hemmed in."

"Rachel, I'd like to ask you just a few questions."

"Yes, ma'am."

"The 'ma'am' won't be necessary. Why do you always say 'ma'am,' by the way?"

"My parents told me to. And they liked it at the school I used to go to."

"Well," she said with a smile, "you'll find us a lot less formal here at North Place. Now, I want to tell you that a very serious thing has happened."

"Yes, Miss Pick."

"A girl has run away from school. Her name is

Carlisle Daggett. She was in your room at the infirmary the night you were hit with a hockey ball."

"I know."

"Rachel, do you know what it means when a young person is said to be a delinquent?"

"Like the Silks and the Emperors."

"The Silks and the Emperors?"

"Street gangs. They're active in Coney Island."

"Well, yes. It's the same thing. Now I want to tell you a bit about Carlisle Daggett." I nodded and fastened my eyes on Miss Pick. "Carlisle is a bright girl, very bright, but she has in her a streak of destructiveness and willfullness that nobody seems to understand."

"Destructiveness," I said evenly.

"She tried to set fire to a building last year."

"She did?"

"Luckily, she was stopped in time. But had she not been, it could have resulted in the death of many people."

"That's terrible!"

"Carlisle isn't terrible," Miss Pick continued. "She's sick. It's like having any other disease. It's no different from having polio or cerebral palsy except that it affects her mind, not her body."

"Why isn't she in a mental institution then?" I asked.

Miss Pick drew a sharp breath. "Rachel," she said, "I know you've heard something about this by now.

I'll tell you, in full detail, about a certain part of North Place. Over beyond that body of water," she waved toward the moat, "is Quordoset Hall. In it are many girls, bright and talented like yourself; however they don't attend classes with you."

"Why not?"

"Because most of them are girls like Carlisle. They are rebels, and we don't think it's right for them to be with the normal girls. Nevertheless, most of them graduate, and with a doctor's help are able to come out quite nicely by the time they are seniors."

I was about to ask how much it cost to be in Quordoset Hall but decided not to. "I'm glad they do" was all I said.

"Well, I'm glad too, Rachel, and now I'd like to ask you if you realize the gravity of Carlisle's situation."

"The gravity?"

"We have a feeling you went out, Rachel. The nurse checked your bed around midnight. She did not check the other bed, as it was behind a small screen and the girl had been given a strong sedative. Nurse Mott said you were not there. She thought you had gone to the bathroom. Had you?"

I felt all cold and tight inside. "I went out," I said. "I went to the apple orchard."

"And you knew that was against the rules."

"Yes, ma'am."

"Why, Rachel?"

"Because I have to have some time alone. I don't know why, I'm sorry. I can't help it. I promise I'll try to fit in. Please don't bring me up in front of that Honor Court!"

"This time I'll tell you I understand, Rachel, because I do. But you must tell me everything you remember about Carlisle Daggett. Her parents are very anxious and will hold the school responsible if she isn't found."

"All I remember is that she looked kind of fat and curly-headed, and she was sleeping like death, and she wasn't there when I woke up the next morning."

"You didn't say that to Miss Abloi, the first time she asked you."

"I didn't think it was important, Miss Pick."

"All right, how could you? Go on."

"That's all."

"Are you sure?"

"Well, that's all I can remember right now."

"I believe you, Rachel. You may go back to your room. Expect no punishments for your nightly walks. Just try not to do it again, please."

I ran directly to the dorm. Ebbie was not in the room. I took the cigarette pack out of my purse, memorized the address on the inside, and flushed it down the john. About half a mile down the main road from school is a public phone booth. I crawled out my favorite downstairs window and ran the whole distance at top speed. There was a girl using the phone, however, a North Place girl. I laughed to myself and felt a little better. So I was not the only one! Eventually she hung up, and I waited until she was out of sight before emerging from the bushes.

There was no listing in New York City for the name and address Carlisle had given me. I was sure I had it right. I couldn't wait till the weekend to find her. There was only one thing that might work. I called Linda McCarthy.

"Rache! How are you?"

"I'm in trouble. You've got to help me, Lin."

"Trouble!"

I explained the whole situation to her. "I don't know how much they know," I said finally. "They might find out I had coffee with her."

"You'd better tell them."

"But how much should I tell them?"

"You swore to God you wouldn't tell on Carlisle?"

"I did. But mostly I don't want to tell them."

"But if she set a fire!"

"I know, I know. Maybe I'm doing the wrong thing, but I gave my word, Lin."

"Well, you've already lied to the school."

"I guess I have."

"Rache, you've never lied in your whole life!"

"I know it. But I seem to be doing it all the time now."

"Well," said Linda with a sigh, "I guess you want me to go down to the Village and find her."

"Could you, Lin?"

"I'm not allowed, you know, but I'll do it."

"Lin, it's like the cats, remember the cats?"

"What's like the cats?"

"This girl. Even if she did set a fire. If they find her they'll keep her here and she hates it, or worse, she'll go to a reform school."

"It's much worse than the cats in my opinion."

"Lin, thank you so much, I can't tell you. Call me tomorrow night at nine. Emergency, person to person."

"Will do. Hey! When will you be home?"

"Next weekend," I decided suddenly.

"I can't wait!"

I must explain about the cats. Linda has often expressed a desire to go to a certain college in Los Angeles. Apparently they have a big medical laboratory on campus. Linda found out they keep hundreds of cats there in small cages for experimentation purposes. She says they do unimaginably cruel things to them, and that she is going to attend that college one day just to let them out some night. I think that is a fine thing, and a much better motive for going to college than studying English or something. I am falling asleep. Over and out.

## Monday, October 8

Strange feeling that maybe this whole thing will go away. Linda did not call me tonight. Perhaps Carlisle has been found. I'm afraid that in a way I hope she has; it certainly would make my life a lot easier. Perhaps she didn't go to that address at all, or maybe she has moved on, thinking I would rat on her. Still, if Carlisle has not been found, I will never, never tell. The whole thing is so like a chase movie, you begin to root for the victim, no matter what they've done.

Things are slightly more bearable here. Perhaps because I'm too afraid to break any more rules, and Miss Pick has excused me for the ones I have already broken. Today we had a class instead of gym. They call it Hygiene, but it's just the same old sex and drug stuff they give in public schools, which means, of course, Fallopian tubes and marijuana. This is a brand-new teacher, however, a young man, and the course is terribly modern. He calls it Interaction Analysis.

Not only does he teach us, but he says we teach him as well by rating his "communication efficiency" on a scale from one to ten. Each desk is equipped with dials, which are hooked up to a machine in the back of the room. After class he looks at the numbers and finds out how effective a teacher he's been. He claims not to know who is twisting what dial in which direction.

A girl called Faith Simon really got him today. She asked if he was married. Mr. Burger, who seems to blush at every question except those about dope, said no, he wasn't. A bit later, she asked if intercourse was a lot of fun, since it doesn't mention this in our textbook. "Yes, of course," he answered, "if you want to use the word 'fun.'"

"But the book says you shouldn't ever do it before you're married," Faith pressed on.

"Yes, we generally advocate—"

"But how do you know it's so much fun then?" Faith asked. The whole class began to titter, and everybody swung their dials around to zero. Poor Mr. Burger. We all decided, starting next week, to leave our dials at ten all period long. The following week we'll give him a nine, then an eight, and so forth. It's odd, we probably wouldn't give him so much grief if he weren't so nice and didn't sweat so much.

Absolutely nobody joined in the song at the end of the class. He said he had written it himself and it was to be sung to the tune of "The Caissons Go Rolling Along."

Last verse of the Interaction Analysis song:

*What we hope to do*
*Is reveal yourself to you*
*We'll study our learning with this aim.*
  *(tan ta ran ta ta ta)*

*The most direct lass*
*Can lead the rest of the class*
*As we join in the interaction game*
*(tan ta ra)*

That's supposed to make us reveal all our true feelings about sex, our parents, etc. and have a "better relationship with ourselves and our fellow students."

Put in a request slip for this weekend home and called Mother and Dad. (They are very happy I'm coming and so am I. Should I not be? Four days to go.)

## Tuesday, October 9

Once again, nothing happened about Carlisle. No one questioned me. I slipped out tonight and called Linda. She said she'd been trying to get me but couldn't (funny). Linda had gone to the Village and found Carlisle. "She didn't want to see me at first, but then she came out and I was able to talk to her."

"What'd she say? What'd she say?"

"Well," said Linda, "she seemed like a nice girl. She had a bad cold. I asked her if she'd ever set fire to anything."

"What did she say?"

"She said 'Yes, but it wasn't intentional.' It seems she had this huge old closet in her room last year, big enough to walk around in, and she used to sit and smoke in it. One night she was caught by a housemother. Nothing had really caught on fire or anything. She was brought up before the dean and threatened with expulsion, but her old man paid the school off to keep everything quiet. Her old man sounds like a real moneybags!"

"Did you believe her?"

"I don't know. She's funny, hippie type."

"What else did she say?"

"Well, she said she felt awful about burdening you with the responsibility. She said to tear up the pack of cigarettes with the address on it and forget the whole thing happened. I thought that was a good idea."

"But I've memorized the address!"

"Oh, dear!"

"Oh, dear what?"

"Well, I didn't know that. I thought you could just tear up the pack of cigarettes and you wouldn't know the address anymore. Then you could tell the school you had no idea where she was and you wouldn't be lying and she wouldn't get caught."

"What am I going to do?"

"I don't know. Don't do anything until they ask you again." Linda suggested some tricks for forgetting addresses. "Say all sorts of street names and numbers to yourself," she said. I told her it wouldn't work. The address was embedded in my mind. Then she said her father was beginning to listen to the conversation and she had to hang up.

It isn't lying about the address half so much as being caught in a lie that I'm worried about. No, that's wrong. It's Carlisle herself. I sympathize with her terribly. I can see something like this happening to me, and my depending on the word of a stranger. I can't turn her in and that's that.

## Wednesday, October 10

The boom fell completely today. I was called out of Algebra at ten thirty this morning. All of my classes are difficult, but this is the worst of all. I was a little relieved to escape part of the lesson, even though I know it will hurt me in the end. Miss Bruno, the teacher, didn't want to let me go. The girl who had come for me shifted her weight from one foot to the other several times while she listened to Miss Bruno's reasons for not interrupting classes, not spoiling the work of a student who was already behind, etc., etc. At last she agreed, however, and I left class feeling very foolish. "Oy vey!"

I said to the girl as we walked down the hall. "What a creep! I don't see why I have to get a lecture when Miss Abloi herself calls me out of class. It isn't my fault." The girl said nothing but looked very pale.

Miss Abloi greeted me very pleasantly. She asked me please to sit and wait while she ruffled through a stack of papers on her desk. Then, with her glasses perched on the end of her nose, she swallowed hard and said, "Rachel, I'm afraid we have some rather alarming news."

"WHAT?" I asked, terrified that my mother or father had died.

"Well, it seems that the gentleman who runs the coffee shop in the bus terminal in Boston remembers seeing Carlisle Daggett having coffee with another young lady last Wednesday night." Miss Abloi pushed back her spectacles and ruffled through the papers once more, as if this bit of information was not to concern me.

"Yes?" I said, biting off a hangnail.

"Well, of course we asked for a description of the other young lady and it turns out that that description sounds a great deal like you. We can't be sure, of course."

"Well, of course."

"But we thought we had better ask you first."

"Ask me?"

"Yes. We've arranged that the gentleman should come up to the school this afternoon and view the student body, just to see if the girl he saw last Wednesday night is among them. However, if you tell us it was indeed you, that won't be necessary."

"It won't be."

"It won't be what?"

"Necessary. It was me."

"Rachel, why didn't you tell us? We've wasted days looking for Carlisle Daggett. If you'd have told us in the first place, we would have known where she was!"

"I don't know where she is."

"I didn't ask you that. I asked you why you didn't tell us that you had coffee with her."

"Well, I was going to, but I was afraid."

"You told Miss Pick you had gone to the apple orchard, and she excused you from discipline. Could you not have told her then where you really went?"

"I was afraid."

"Do you intend to continue breaking rules that everyone else must obey?"

"No, ma'am."

"NO, MISS ABLOI!"

"I'm sorry. No, Miss Abloi. I've resolved to start doing better. Ever since my talk with Miss Pick I haven't broken a single rule."

"Do you know the punishment waiting for you if you were to be disciplined for the rules you've already broken?"

"About the limit, I expect."

"Just about the limit, and you've been here only a week."

"Are you, are you going to—"

"No. Not if you make me a solemn promise to tell everything you know about Carlisle Daggett. Absolutely everything that happened and everything she said. You will have a clean slate."

"Well, I went to the city with her. We sneaked out the bathroom window in the infirmary. She told me she'd been in the bars in town last year, but I said I wouldn't go into one because my parents would be angry. We went to the coffee shop. She asked me if I wanted to run away with her. I said no, I wanted to stay in school. She said good-bye and left on a bus."

"What bus did she take?"

"It was a Greyhound, I think."

"Rachel, *only* Greyhound buses were leaving at that hour."

"That's what I said, a Greyhound bus."

"Rachel, there were three buses leaving around that time. One for Chicago, one for New York, and one for Miami. Which bus did Carlisle take?"

I screwed up my face as if I were trying to remember, but I don't think this fooled Miss Abloi. "She said something about a place with a lot of kids. Three girls and two boys and the girl was over twenty, one of them, I mean. Nothing more than that."

"But which city?"

"I don't remember."

"You *must* remember!"

"I'm sorry. I just don't remember, Miss Abloi. I don't want to give you a false lead."

"You have given us enough false leads already," she said. "You may leave now, but I urge you to think very hard. North Place has been lenient with you, and now you must be fair with us."

"I'm trying," I said, getting red in the face. "I've told you everything I know."

"Rachel, sit down."

I sat.

"I understand that you were not in attendance the first night of school when we had our get-together."

"I was with Miss Block. Miss Block will verify that."

"I believe you, I believe you," said Miss Abloi.

"I *was*," I insisted again.

"I believe you, Rachel," said Miss Abloi, "whenever you are fierce. You were just very fierce. You give everything away in your face. Had you attended the lecture Sunday night, however, you might have learned something very valuable about our honor code here at North Place. Namely, that it is not pleasant to have to report on oneself or one's fellow students, but it is necessary. If we are all to enjoy our freedom, then we must have our responsibilities. We do not treat you like children here at North Place, nor do we expect to be treated like parents who are lied to."

"I don't *know* where Carlisle Daggett is! I've told you all I know!" I said, as fiercely as I could.

"That is what you said before. But I urge you to reconsider everything. Now go back to your Algebra class. I understand from Miss Bruno that you are far behind the rest of the girls."

I left quickly, unable to eat lunch or concentrate on anything except talking to Carlisle this weekend. I could not contrive to get into another accident in hockey and didn't dare sneak out to the phone booth again.

## Thursday, October 11

Received a pink slip on my breakfast plate today: RE-PORT TO HONOR COURT AT 4:45 P.M. I had to wait almost an hour before they called me in. In the meantime the waiting room was full of girls I had never seen. Each time someone came into the room, I raised my head with a jerk, as if I expected a familiar face, but I can't say whose.

I asked the girl sitting on my right what she was in for.

"Cribbing," she said.

"Cribbing?"

"Cheating on an exam. I had it written in the palm of my hand and they caught me."

I must say, cheating has never occurred to me, and I almost congratulated myself for not doing anything as obviously untruthful as that. But I wonder if what I am doing isn't worse. Am I wrong?

"I should have known better," the girl continued. "I should have written the answers on a Kleenex or inscribed them into the desk the day before."

"They'd probably still have caught you," I remarked, "if they're on the lookout."

"Oh, they're always on the lookout." She sighed. "Next time I'll write my notes on Lifesavers and eat them as I go."

"Marty Robbins," said a voice from the door. The girl went in and emerged five minutes later looking much relieved.

"What did they give you?" I asked.

"Twenty chits," she said mournfully. "Lost a weekend but I'll do the Gettysburgs."

"Rachel Saseekian," said the same voice from inside the door.

There were twelve girls sitting around a table, all upperclassmen and all quite grown-up looking. Shiny hair, turned up noses. No uniforms, as these aren't required in the upper school after class. One girl had long stringy black hair and was wearing blue jeans. She was knitting voraciously and did not look up. Two teachers sat on the sidelines. "Good afternoon," said the head girl. The floor shifted under my feet. I thought it would swallow me up like quicksand. "Well?" she said, since I had not answered.

"Well?" I replied inaudibly.

"We understand you have something to tell us," she continued, after clearing her throat.

"But *you* asked *me* to come here."

"Do you not have something to tell us?"

"I don't know."

"Well . . ." she repeated very slowly, looking at the teachers and the other girls.

I decided the best thing to do was to break down and cry. I admitted the nightly walks to the moat and the orchard, all the lies I had told about going for coffee with Carlisle, every rule I could think of that I had broken. "I put myself at the mercy of this court!" I said between sobs. (I read that, I think, in a Perry Mason book.)

They told me to wait in another room for a few minutes. They deliberated, and when I was allowed back in the room, told me that they had fined me twenty chits and one weekend.

"What does that mean?" I asked.

"That means you can make up the chits with Gettysburg Addresses, but not the weekend." said the head girl.

I panicked. "You mean I can't go home this week-end?"

"Not until Thanksgiving, I'm afraid," she said, "but it's only seven weeks."

"Even if I write five hundred Gettysburg Addresses?"

"NO!" she said. "Marcia Black!"

Marcia Black came lumbering into the room, and I was led out firmly by the shoulder.

Somehow I made it back to my room. Ebbie was there, fidgeting.

"I thought you were on Honor Court," I said.

"I am, but you sit out if your roommate is involved. How did it go?"

"I have to go home this weekend. I just *have* to."

"Why?"

"I promised. I promised to see Pete."

"Well, I guess you can't," said Ebbie, fingering the lipsticks on her bureau.

"But I have to talk to him."

"You can call him, can't you?"

"They listen. You told me they listen in."

"Not always. Besides, all you have to say is you won't be seeing him."

"Look, Ebbie, can I tell you something very personal?"

"Of course," she said, wide-eyed, and sat right down next to me on the bed.

"I'm afraid I might be— I mean I haven't had my period in over six weeks and I'm afraid I might—"

"No!" she whispered, clapping her hand over her mouth in amazement. "You *didn't!*"

"Well, I don't know if I did or not. I didn't *want* to."

"Jesus Christ! I had you figured for a virgin till you were thirty-five!"

"Well, I still might be. I mean I'm just worried and I wanted to talk to Pete."

"God!" she said. "God!"

"Well, that's what happens in public schools," I sighed. "Believe me I'll never do it again though."

"Well, look," Ebbie said. "There's a phone booth down the road about half a mile. If you want to sneak out, I'll look the other way."

I made my way as quickly as possible out the back window of the dorm and dashed through the woods to the phone booth. A man was talking for what seemed like an hour before I could call.

I told my mother I was in trouble, but couldn't say what kind.

"Rachel, what have you done?" she asked, horrified.

"I want you to trust me."

"I trust you, but what have you done?"

"Mother, please! I don't have much time. I want you to please do something for me. I want you to please call the school and say my grandmother has just died or something. I have to be back Saturday for the funeral, for the weekend. Say we have to drive to Philadelphia."

"What?"

"Please, Mother. Do it for me. I'll explain later."

"But why? Aren't you coming home anyway?"

"No. They took my weekend away. Please!"

"Rachel, what have you done?"

"Will you trust me to tell you when I get home?"

Here there was a great deal of mumbling and my father got on the phone. I went through the same conversation with him.

"Are you getting yourself kicked out, young lady?"

"No, Daddy."

"Then what's all this stuff about funerals?"

"Please, Daddy, trust me."

There was a silence and he said, "O.K., we'll do it, but it had better be worth it."

"Oh, Daddy, thank you," I gasped.

Ebbie was very kind when I got back to the room. "I was a little nervous you wouldn't make it back for dinner," she said, putting her wristwatch on the bureau, "and then they'd ask me where you were, and—You should have told me earlier, though, I mean about your predicament. No wonder you've been nervous and sneaking out all the time and everything. Have you seen a doctor?"

"No, I haven't seen a doctor."

"Well, you ought to go to a doctor. I know a good one here in Boston who does just that sort of thing."

"I guess I'll tell my parents and go to my own doctor," I said.

"*Don't* tell your parents!" said Ebbie. "On the other hand, you're awfully young, maybe you should. I just can't get over it. I hardly believed you when you said you had a boyfriend. I guess you're pretty normal after all."

"Normal! What do you mean, 'normal'?"

"Well, like I really didn't like you too much before, because, well, you know. I mean the piano and breaking all the rules like they didn't apply to you, and stuff, and not getting to know anybody and things, but I mean, I want to tell you that I understand now. I mean about everything."

(Play it to the hilt, Rachel.) "Well I'm glad I told somebody at last," I said with an earnest sigh.

"Gee, how did it happen? I mean did he make you do it and stuff? Was it in a car?"

"No. It was at his house. His parents weren't home."

"In a real bed?"

"I'd rather not think about it," I muttered.

"God!" said Ebbie.

"Please, let's not talk about it anymore."

"Well, gee. I'm sorry. We won't talk about it anymore," said Ebbie. "But, I mean, if you find out you are, and stuff, are you going to keep the baby?"

"Ebbie, I don't know. I don't even know if I'm pregnant yet, so let's just wait and see."

"Well, if you need any money, I have five thousand dollars in my bank."

I thanked her very much and went to dinner. I'm finishing this in the john, as usual, sitting on the edge of a tub, worrying about what I'm going to say to Carlisle and my parents. Ebbie Faber has FIVE THOUSAND DOLLARS IN HER BANK! FIVE THOUSAND DOLLARS! HER BANK!

## Friday, October 12

Miss Sampson caught me dreaming in English class today. She pointed with a rubber-tipped stick to a motto, written in Old English script above the blackboard. "Theirs not to reason why, Theirs but to do or die" it says.

"What does this mean to you, Rachel?" asked Miss Sampson, snapping me out of the daydream.

" 'Charge of the Light Brigade,' " I said, stunned. "Alfred Lord Tennyson."

"I didn't ask you who wrote it, I asked you what it meant to you."

"Well, I guess it means they all died," I said. General giggles in the classroom.

"Rachel, you seem to know Tennyson very well," Miss Sampson continued, mad as hops at something.

"Well, no. It's just one of my father's favorite poems and he's read it to me."

"And would you like to recite the whole poem for the class?"

"I don't know the whole thing by heart, ma'am."

"In other words," she said, "you know just these two lines, just enough to impress your classmates."

"I wasn't trying—" I began, but there was a gentle tap on the door, and the messenger girl from two days ago told Miss Sampson that I was to go to Miss Pick's office.

"Over the weekend, Rachel," said Miss Sampson, "you might memorize the rest of 'The Charge of the Light Brigade.'"

"Yes, ma'am."

"YES, MISS SAMPSON!"

I was kept waiting for ten minutes in an outer office. The woman typing at the reception desk said nothing, never even acknowledged my presence. Eventually she piled up her papers, separating carbons from noncarbons, and disappeared with a little sigh around a corner.

I tried Linda's method for forgetting things. "Thirty-four Greenwich Avenue, 1237 MacDougal Street, 8½ Thompson Street," I whispered to myself, with my eyes shut. It didn't work, but Miss Pick caught me right in the middle.

"Come in, Rachel," she said.

I jumped up, and there were my parents.

"I'll leave you now," said Miss Pick.

"Rachel," my mother began, "Miss Pick has told us everything, and we're ashamed of you!"

"Everything?"

"Everything."

I drew a deep breath and expected to cry, but I didn't for once. Neither was the invisible hand there. I faced them squarely and asked, "What do you think I should do?"

"First of all," said Daddy, twirling his hat between his knees, "you've got to tell us where this girl is."

"You have never in your whole life been a liar," interrupted my mother. "Never once! I don't understand this at all."

"Let her finish," said Daddy.

"I don't know where the girl is."

"Rachel, you're not telling the truth," Mother said.

"You didn't tell the truth either. You said you'd let me come home this weekend. You didn't say anything about coming here and talking to Miss Pick."

"We called Miss Pick," said Daddy. "We told her we had a family emergency. She was extremely kind and agreed to let you go home. But she said she'd like to talk to us here, before you left. We couldn't refuse."

"Oh."

"Well?"

"I can't talk to you here."

"Why not?" Mother asked.

"Are you going to take me home?"

"Of course we're going to take you home. We can't very well tell Miss Pick the emergency is over. Rachel, you've trapped *us* in lies as well as yourself."

"But I haven't meant to trap anybody. I'm the one most trapped."

Daddy looked at the ceiling. "Well, it's very easy to get yourself out," he said. "All you have to do is tell the truth."

"I have told the truth!"

"I don't think you've told all of it."

I said nothing.

"Rachel, do you or do you not know where this girl is?"

"No!" I said loudly and raised my finger to my lips, looking pleadingly at both of them. My mother was about to say something when Daddy took her by the arm and rose. "Come along then," he said gruffly.

Miss Pick was not outside the door listening, as I had supposed. She was nowhere in sight. I walked silently through the office corridors with my parents and climbed into the back seat of the car. They had not brought Swamp with them. Daddy started the car, and Mother spun around in her seat. "Now you can tell us," she said. "Where is this girl?" I didn't answer.

"Rachel, do you understand what this means? Not

only for you and your whole future, but for this silly girl too?"

"Enough!" said my father, and I sighed with relief. The rest of the ride home I slept, waking every now and then in a small panic. I decided, finally, at a toll-booth that I would just go and find Carlisle and tell her I had to inform, although I didn't quite know how to manage a trip to the Village. I'm not supposed to go there and don't want to lie to my parents.

Dinner was a disaster. Mother was afraid to say anything for fear of being shut up by Daddy, and Daddy didn't want to push me, I could see. The whole scene sat like a lump of clay on my head.

"Otherwise," he began, in the middle of a long silence, "how do you like school?"

"I hate it."

"Rachel, how could you hate it after only two weeks?" my Mother asked anxiously.

"Mother, I'm sorry, but all the girls, well, they're all so rich and strange."

"What's strange about them?"

"Well, my roommate, Ebbie Faber, she's always trying to get me to like popular music and boys."

"That doesn't sound any different from the kids who go to Brighton Beach High," said my father.

"Well, it isn't, except they're all like that. And I don't have any freedom, that's the worst part. One hour and a quarter a day, and even then, people are always around."

"You don't want to grow up to be a hermit, do you?" Mother asked.

"Mother, I just want to live at home and go to school with my own friends and not be treated like some kind of prisoner!"

That stopped them for a minute.

"How are your studies?" asked my father.

"Terrible. I'm doing terribly!"

"Do you do your homework?"

"Yes, I do my homework, but I can't concentrate. I'm just miserable. So *what* about Algebra and all that crap anyway!"

"Rachel, you may leave the table," Mother said.

Daddy came into my room about eleven thirty. I wished I'd gone to bed so he wouldn't have bothered me, but there I was, sitting in my chair picking my toenails.

"Well!" he said, collapsing into the other chair.

"I don't know where she is," I said quickly.

"I never said you did. Just tell me what's going on."

I told him as much as I could about school and about Carlisle. When I got to the part about the reform school, he laughed uproariously. "I hope you don't believe that for a minute!" he said.

"I didn't at first, but I do now."

"That's ridiculous, honey. People don't send their own children to reform schools, especially nice families."

"Maybe they're not such a nice family. Maybe if Carlisle is as sick as everyone says she is, her parents are terrible people."

"They may not be the best of parents," said Daddy, swirling a beer around in a glass, "but if they're as well off as you say they are, I can tell you they won't have any daughter in a reform school."

I picked a toenail very carefully and didn't answer.

"Honey, I don't blame you a bit for feeling sorry for the girl. She probably made you promise not to tell where she was. But this reform-school business! Don't you see that that is part of her problem? That's what makes her sick? She's got to be under responsible, professional care."

"All right, so?"

"Honey, I want to believe you, really, I do. But you must realize what you're doing by holding this back."

"I realize."

He looked at me out of half-closed eyes for a second and then put his hands in his pockets and got up to leave. "O.K.," he said.

"Daddy!"

"Yes?"

"Nothing." I went back to my toenails.

## Saturday, October 13

First thing this morning I stopped and saw Linda. We walked up and down the street talking the whole thing over and concluded only that she was glad she was not in my shoes. She also told me a lot about high school, about my friends and what they were doing. "I wish I were there," I said wistfully.

"But it's so easy!" said Linda. "All you have to do is tell them you refuse to say where Carlisle is because you made a promise, then they'll kick you out of boarding school, and you can go to school with us!"

"No," I said. "I'd only get into more trouble with her parents and the police and stuff."

"Well, it still seems like an easy thing for you to get kicked out."

"But I don't want to get kicked out."

"Why not?"

"Because of all the money my parents spent. I feel I have to live up to something and not be a coward. Besides, it would be a black mark on my record."

Linda kicked a stone.

I managed to take the right subways, after asking directions at least three times from the conductors and token sellers. No disastrous attacks occurred, although I hadn't told Mother and Dad I was going to the Village.

## GIRL MOWED DOWN BY IRT

### PRIVATE SCHOOL TEEN-AGER FOUND
### DEAD IN VILLAGE—PARENTS GRIEVE

ran the *Daily News* headlines in my imagination.

Carlisle was sitting in a frayed sling chair when a boy finally let me into the apartment. She jumped when she saw me and wildly started to straighten up her hair.

"Rachel!" she said. "You split! You've come to stay!" She was faking that. I think she knew right away why I had come.

"No, I haven't split," I said, trying to sit on the window sill. The floor was horribly dirty and there was no furniture in the room save Carlisle's chair. "But I'm in bad trouble, Carlisle. I'm afraid I'm going to have to tell them where you are."

Carlisle said nothing but blew her nose a couple of times. "Look," I continued nervously, "they found the coffee-shop man, the waiter. He can identify me. So far, I haven't told them which bus you took, but I'm afraid they're going to get it out of me. If they don't, my father will."

"Rachel, why don't you forget them and come and live with us? Don't you see how they're hanging you up?"

"Carlisle, I'm only thirteen years old! Besides, I don't *want* to!"

"Do you want to stay in that school, where they treat you like the Spanish Inquisition?"

"Carlisle, please, can't you find another place to stay? A place I don't know about?"

Carlisle folded up her handkerchief and put it on the floor. She seemed to have a very bad cold. "O.K., O.K., let me think a minute," she mumbled.

"Just move on, just don't tell me where you're going!"

"Just move on? Rachel, I'm happy here," she said angrily. "I don't have any other place to go. Why was I so stupid as to tell a little twerp like you?"

"It isn't my fault! I didn't tell them a thing. They found it all out for themselves, and if I'd have denied it, it wouldn't have done any good anyway. I think you're lucky I haven't told them any more than I have!"

"I'm sorry," she sniffed. "I didn't mean that. You've been great. But I don't know where to go. I can't just stay on the street; they'd pick me up sooner or later. Did I tell you I was going to school here?"

"School?"

"Yeah, N.Y.U. It's great."

"But how can you get into college when you haven't even graduated from high school?"

"A girl I met down here," she explained. "She left for Mexico. Couldn't hack school anymore, but she was signed up for her whole freshman year, paid for and everything. I just go to her classes. The place is so big the professors don't know the difference."

"But you won't get credit for it. You can't use it toward a degree," I said.

"Who needs degrees?" said Carlisle. "It's something to do and I'm enjoying it. I'm also working part-time in a photography lab."

"Is that really true about the reform school?"

"*Yes!*"

"Well, I don't know."

"Listen, Rachel, please understand. All I want is for everyone to leave me alone. Leave me in peace and let me go my own way. I don't want to go to North Place. I'd die in a reformatory and I can't be anywhere near my parents. Don't you see?"

There, she'd said it. I felt myself buckling again, because of course I knew exactly how she felt, and I didn't want to turn her in at all.

"I just don't know what to do," she said wretchedly. "I should have just disappeared and never told anyone. Then all this would never have happened."

"I'll try not to tell," I said, getting off the window sill.

"Do you believe me now, about the reform school, I mean?"

"I just don't know, Carlisle. I do believe you have the right to live your own life though."

Suddenly she shoved both her arms at me. I had no idea what she was doing, and I stepped back instantly. "What— is there something wrong?" I asked.

"Look!" she said. There was nothing at all there. "Don't you see?"

"No," I admitted.

"Don't you see those stitches on my wrists?"

"Yes."

"Well, what the hell do you think they're from?"

"An accident? A car maybe?"

"It wasn't any accident!" she said, almost in tears, and turned her back.

"Good-bye," I said. "I hope I don't have to tell, Carlisle." She didn't say good-bye. Only stared moodily out the window, blowing her nose on the bandanna again. I noticed she was wearing the same dress she'd had on when she left North Place. Perhaps she hasn't any clothes.

Mother wasn't home when I got back to the house, and Daddy hardly looked up as I flew through the living room. As I began climbing the stairs he chuckled. "Still haven't made up your mind, eh?"

"What do you mean?" I asked.

"Did you see the girl?"

"I don't know what you mean."

"You wear it all over your face."

"Maybe you don't know everything!" I said and started flouncing up the stairs again.

Dad called after me, "Do whatever you think is right, honey, but remember, if you give up this chance for a silly little lying dope of a girl, you'll have to live with it."

"Who says she's a dope?"

Much more gently he said, "I meant that within a context, honey. We all make mistakes, and it's a pity to make a big one when you're very young. At least let's talk this over."

"There's nothing to talk about."

"Rachel, I know you know where this girl is. I know you saw her today. I even made sure your mother didn't make a fuss about where you were going this morning. But North Place knows this too. If you will make amends now, they will forgive you and understand. I've already spoken to Miss Pick about this. But if you don't, you're being very foolish. You must remember you are only thirteen years old and don't know everything yet. No one expects you to, so you should at least talk this out with someone.

"I don't *know* where she is. I spent the day just thinking, that's all."

"Thinking about what?"

"*Thinking!*"

"If you don't know where she is, and you're not holding something back, you wouldn't have to think about it, would you?"

"Daddy, please!"

"Determined, aren't you?"

"Can I ask you something?"

"Of course."

"What does it mean when someone has scars on their wrists?"

"It means they've tried to take their own life."

"Oh."

## Sunday, October 14

Total stubbornness on my part. They drove me back to school and I said good-bye coldly. I'm back now in the dormitory john writing. No one here has said a thing. I still haven't made up my mind. Funny, a real choice to make now, and no Choice Genie to make it easy.

## Monday, October 15

Another pink slip appeared on my breakfast plate today, lying there like a fried egg. School was interminable this morning. I'd forgotten to memorize "The Charge of the Light Brigade," and Miss Sampson gave me hell. I skipped activity period and lunch and just went walking in the woods, another breach of the rules, but I don't care anymore. If they wanted to kick me out, they'd do it for not ratting on Carlisle and forget about walks in the woods. I picked a flower and put it in back of my ear for luck.

At 4:45 Honor Court convened. I was the only girl waiting. The group of girls was the same, but both Miss Pick and Miss Abloi were present this time. Miss Pick sat off a little to the side, one of her feet tapping in time, as if there were music playing.

"We all know why you're here, Rachel," the head girl began. She cleared her throat and looked over at Miss Pick, but Miss Pick only stared out of focus at something.

"I've told you everything," I said, since it seemed to be my turn. It was easy to say that suddenly. All the agonizing subsided within me, and I found I had made up my mind at last.

"Are you saying that you went and had coffee with

Carlisle, had at least an hour and a half conversation with her, and you do not know where she was going? Not even the city she had in mind?"

"Yes."

"Rachel, do you value your status here at North Place?"

"My status?"

"Do you want to stay with us?"

"Yes, very much," I answered with my eyes lowered. Twelve stock-still girls fastened their eyes on me. Even the one in blue jeans had stopped her knitting for this occasion. A fly buzzed past the head girl's ear and she brushed it on by. Shiny red hair, a turned-up freckled nose, and glasses that kept reflecting the overhead lights so that I couldn't see her eyes. I don't know her name, but I'll call her Marjorie, because she was wearing a fat blue-quilted jumper with brass buttons and looked like a Marjorie.

"If you tell us a single lie in the course of these proceedings, you will be dismissed from the student body."

"I am not a liar," I said angrily.

"O.K., Rachel, nobody said you were. We also realize you have been under considerable strain this past week, and that it is not as easy for you to get along here as it might be for another girl."

"I don't know what you mean," I said.

"Well, for example, Miss Pick has told us you would like to change your schedule. You would like more time to play the piano, for instance. That's perfectly admirable and understandable. There's no reason why you shouldn't be allowed to do that, considering your talent. (That word again.) That's what I mean about its not being easy for you." Marjorie giggled a little and adjusted her glasses. "Perhaps North Place should be a little more flexible with talented people."

"Well, thank you," I mumbled. I shot a glance at Miss Pick, but she still seemed to be somewhere else. She was gazing out the window this time.

Marjorie continued, "You have been given twenty chits and lost your weekend home, I believe?"

"Yes."

"Well, we feel that that was perhaps a bit unjust, considering. So we have reinstated the weekend and dropped the chits."

"But I already took my weekend yesterday."

"That was a family emergency. You still have another weekend left this term."

"Oh. Well, thank you."

"You see, Rachel, we feel you should have a completely clean slate. Forget all about the past. We don't think you'll want to stay with us if you think we are repressive. You have come to us with a very different background from most of the girls here and maybe we've been unwise in regimenting you so strongly. In other words Miss Pick and Miss Abloi and some of your teachers have gotten together with us and had a talk. We've decided that this thing with Carlisle Daggett had caused you much distress but that also you are unhappy with North Place in general, and we want you to be happy here. I think if we give a little, and you give a little—"

"Of course," I said. My head was very muddled. "You mean you're going to allow me free time and stuff?"

She nodded. "There has also been a policy change regarding religion. This, of course, was decided by the administration. There are three other girls of the Jewish faith in the student body. None of you will now be required to go to vespers. You may use that hour for whatever you wish. Perhaps you would like to have a Jewish study group, or you could arrange that for your activity hour. There's no reason why you should have to play operetta music if you'd prefer classical."

"Of course."

"Will you give North Place a chance, Rachel?"

"Will I—I?"

"Nothing is keeping you here."

"Well, yes. I mean, yes, of course."

"Good!" Marjorie smiled. "Now. We have been able to find out that a woman, a Mrs. Abberley, was on the bus with Carlisle Daggett. It was the New York bus, by the way. She saw you and Carlisle at the bus station when Carlisle boarded. She says she thinks she saw Carlisle hand you something."

"A pack of cigarettes."

"I see. What did you do with the cigarettes?"

"I threw them out. They're against the rules."

"Well, now, just for the record, let's go over what Carlisle said to you in the bus station. Perhaps there is something we've overlooked."

I took a deep breath. "She told me she was made a special. I asked her what that meant. She explained that she had broken all kinds of rules, had a boy in her room, was caught smoking, that she ran around naked with her organs painted all over her in oil paint. She said her parents had paid the school a lot of money to get her off the hook each time. Finally she messed up a poem in English class and they made her live in Quordoset Hall with all the geniuses and cretins. She said she was going to live with some kids and would I like to come?"

"And you said—"

"I said No. I wanted to attempt to get through North Place."

"And what did Carlisle say to that?"

"She said she expected to see me in about a month because it was so awful here. She doubted if I'd hold out."

"If she said that, didn't she tell you where? Didn't she mention an address?"

"No."

"And she gave you a pack of cigarettes."

"Yes."

"Do you smoke cigarettes?"

"No."

"Then why did she give you a pack of cigarettes?"

"I don't know."

"There must have been a reason, Rachel."

I was beginning to tremble. "The address was on the inside of the cigarette pack. But I swear I didn't look at it! I didn't want to know."

"And in other words," said Marjorie primly, "you foresaw the trouble this would cause and you threw the pack away."

"Maybe. I just didn't want to know. I wanted to forget the whole thing."

"Did she tell you anything else?"

"She said her father would send her to a reform school if she was caught in any trouble again."

"And you believed her."

"Not at first, but I did later."

"Did she tell you she had started a fire in the school last year?"

"Well, she said she'd been caught smoking in a closet, but that no fire had been started. Then she was made a special for lousing up a poem in English."

"You've told us that."

"I guess I have."

"Miss Pick," said Marjorie, turning and gesturing ever so slightly with her right hand, "did Rachel mention the pack of cigarettes to you at any time? Did she say she actually accompanied Carlisle to the bus?"

"No," said Miss Pick, "she didn't."

"I'm sorry," I interrupted, flushing. "I just didn't think that was important."

"Not important?" said Miss Pick, getting to her feet. "Not important! she gave you her address and you threw it away without looking at it and you think that isn't *important*?"

"Well if I don't know where she is anyway, what difference does it make if she gave it to me or not?"

Marjories melted into a seat. Miss Pick seemed to grow taller every second, but her voice was quiet. "Rachel, is that absolutely all you remember?"

"That's all."

"You're not lying to us?"

"No."

"Rachel, are you really Jewish? Did you make a religious conversion without even telling your parents?"

"I guess not."

"Is your father, by any chance, Norman Mailer?"

"No. I guess I made that up too."

"Is your father a Frenchman, Rachel?"

"No."

"Did you really have a family emergency this weekend or did you go to see Carlisle? Or did you see a doctor, as Ebbie said you were, to find out if you were pregnant, when your medical record from your own doctor shows that you haven't even had your first period yet!"

"NO! NO! NO! It's all lies! I'm sorry— Please don't ask me any more." I shut my eyes and tried to stay in the room without breaking into hysterics. I concentrated on a picture of Carlisle, back turned toward me, blowing her nose and looking out the window.

"Well, it seems to me," said Miss Pick quietly, "that you have managed to tell a great many lies in the past two weeks."

I didn't answer.

"Are you aware, Rachel, that Mr. and Mrs. Robert Daggett intend to sue the school for a great deal of money? Even if we are not entirely responsible, it will be a very nasty court case and will get into the papers. Also that Carlisle should be under a doctor's care, before she does something really harmful to herself or others?"

"I'm aware."

"But you persist."

"Miss Pick, I don't *know* where Carlisle is!"

"You expect us to believe that in the face of all the lies you've told us?"

"Yes!"

"Very well." Miss Pick fished around in a drawer. "We have found this, however, I'm sorry to say." She held up my diary. "In between the covers of the *Count of Monte Cristo*, of all things."

"Ebbie!" I shouted. "Ebbie stole that!"

"Rachel, no one has stolen it. We are going to give it back to you, but it behooves us to make every effort to find Carlisle, and this diary was brought to my attention only an hour ago, so we are going to have to look through it, just to see if you've written down the address somewhere."

"You took my diary?"

"As I said, we haven't read it."

"There are many private things in that book," I shouted, "but I guarantee you won't find Carlisle's address!"

"Well, Rachel, if you were in our place, wouldn't you check to make sure?"

"I would never read anything personal of somebody's!"

"Do you want the diary back, Rachel?"

"Yes."

Miss Pick handed it over to me.

"Four thirty-six Bleecker Street, apartment 2D," I said.

Miss Block was sitting on the sofa, just as she had been the first night, when I drifted into the library after dinner.

"I came to say good-bye."

"You're leaving us?"

"You heard about this afternoon?"

"I did."

"My father called. He's picking me up tonight. He and Mother decided last night to let me come home. I didn't even know."

Miss Block heaved a sigh and put down her book.

"Miss Block," I asked, "did I do the right thing?"

"I don't know," she said, and she put her arms around me. For once I didn't mind being touched.

Rosemary Wells' own brief career at boarding school provided her with the inspiration for *The Fog Comes on Little Pig Feet,* her first novel. She is already at work on a second.

Until now Mrs. Wells has been best known for her picture books, among them *Unfortunately Harriet* and *Miranda's Pilgrims.* She has also illustrated many books by other authors, including *Marvin's Manhole; Impossible, Possum;* and *Hungry Fred.*

Born in New York, Mrs. Wells grew up in New Jersey and studied art at the Museum School in Boston. She now lives with her husband in Croton-on-Hudson, New York.